THE
INCAPABILITY
TO CREATE

THE
INCAPABILITY
TO CREATE

AMARA TURNER

THE INCAPABILITY TO CREATE

iUniverse books may be ordered through booksellers or by contacting:

iUniverse
1663 Liberty Drive
Bloomington, IN 47403
www.iuniverse.com
844-349-9409

ISBN: 978-1-6632-0951-1 (sc)
ISBN: 978-1-6632-0952-8 (e)

Library of Congress Control Number: 2021907510

Print information available on the last page.

iUniverse rev. date: 04/09/2021

This work is dedicated to my father. He is an honorable man who stood behind me and fought for me in my darkest hours. This same man who served his country in the marine corps and protected his community. He fathered three military sons, a daughter dedicated to striving for children in need of a better life, and me with a passion for writing.

CHAPTER ONE

HOMECOMING

THE WHITE LIGHT FILLED THE room, stealing my ability to see. I screamed and banged on the door helplessly begging. I can't see. The floor began to open up and only then did the door swing open with such force that it came off entirely. Sweat filled my palms. I have to run. As I am about to reach the threshold, the floor caves in and I fall through, only catching a glimpse of the silhouette standing in the doorway. My screams are swallowed by the blackness that engulfs me as I fall freely into the hole that entrapped me. "Wake up!"

"Julia, wake up you're dreaming."

I sat up quickly and held my hand over my heart as I felt it pounding violently. My breathing was more than erratic and my palms drowning in a pool of sweat. That nightmare is starting to become a problem for me. It almost feels so familiar though. A part of me dares to imagine it being more than a dream. Possibly a memory, and that man. Who is he? He's strangely familiar as well. Regardless of how much these feelings plagued me, it didn't matter, at least not now.

"Julia, are you alright?"

"Hmm? Oh, yeah I'm okay, Salem. It's just a bad dream. Thank you for waking me up."

"Right, well, your break is over. If you need a second to pull yourself together then by all means take another 5 or 10 minutes but do it quickly. Your session with Ezekial is supposed to begin soon."

Salem has always been a good friend to me. She seems a bit annoyed today though. Who wouldn't be? She constantly has to deal with delusional people. Out of all the things on this earth that I could have chosen to do for a living, I decided to work at a psychiatric hospital. I could have done so many other things with my psychology degree. Today won't be an easy session. Salem told me all about Ezekial's episode yesterday. He was doing so well too. It's truly a shame.

The hairs on my neck pricked up as I was making tea. A shadow appeared in the corner of my eye, pacing back and forth. The different shades of black engulfed my peripheral vision, making it difficult for me to dismiss. Didn't Salem leave though? I turned back only to catch a couple of long grey coats on the rack swinging lightly. Must be a draft. As a comfort to myself, I blamed the illusion on my sleep deprivation. Maybe I should get some sleeping pills from my doctor. The same nightmares that haunt me in my sleep are seemingly spilling over into the long days, consequently disturbing my daily rhythm. I stirred my tea as the clanking of the spoon from my mug pierced my ears and began to sip in the warm liquid that soothed my dry throat. Reluctantly, I forced myself to walk towards my office, the therapy room, as my feet drug against the floor in protest.

Out of all the colors they could have picked to paint this psych hospital, they chose to fill the rooms and hallways with grey. Those shades only reflected a depressive state in an already depressing building. I turned left to go down the hall that would lead to my office. This is the hallway where the light would always flicker due to the lack of maintenance and the echoes of the patients screaming persisted during the long hours. It was also the longest hallway in the building giving the illusion that once you started walking, it would take ages to reach the end. It took a good amount of time to get all the way down.

Finally, I reached the therapy room. A soft blue filled the walls allowing the light from the windows to bounce off easily. The floor was still the same tile grey throughout the hospital. My black leather chair sat across from the patient's couch. Although not leather, it's color matched. Footsteps from out the hall lightly pounded against the floor, filling the air with their echoes. I drew a breath in once Salem's words flashed through my mind. With Ezekial's episode yesterday, he would surely be a handful today. The doctors warned me to be careful even though they gave him pills to calm down. A worker stood on the outside of the room and one inside as a safety measure. Trying my best, I cracked a smile while they sat him down.

"Did the man speak to you, Dr. Bettington? He told me he was coming yesterday. He asked me to help him, so I did. I helped him! I did a good job, you know it? He is so proud of me. No! NOT NOW! She doesn't know, I didn't tell her. I wouldn't."

"Ezekial, who are you talking to?'"

"I think you know Dr. Bettington. He came for me just like he is coming for you. He won't stop until you're in the mouse trap with me. Things around you will crumble like a house of cards. He'll start with the whispers and the nightmares. He'll make you feel alone and scared. He'll hurt you like he hurt me. Don't you know it? One day soon, he will drag you with him. He will wake you up and claw his way inside you. Bit by bit, your flesh will tear. You'll scream until you lose your voice. You'll burn in hell! I'm not insane, Dr. Bettington. I'm here because of him."

"Ezekial, you're safe here you know that. There is no man out to get you or me. You're okay. I heard something happened yesterday. Do you want to talk about it?" Poor Ezekial, he looked so sick. His eyes were sunken in and rimmed with a harsh red. His skin was pale as chalk. His back was hunched over, and patches of his hair were missing from his head. He kept pulling it out. He had cuts and bruises along his skin. Every bone in his body protruded out. He looked so sick, so sad, so much in pain,

"Yesterday, the doctor tried to restrain me. I didn't like it. I fought him to the bitter end and for what? For them to drug and restrain me? I was only trying to warn you! I wasn't going to hurt anyone. I don't even deserve to be here. I'm not insane. He just has me."

"Ezekial, I'm sorry they did that to you but you should have asked for me instead of trying to escape your room." His eyes grew wide with every passing second and his shrill voice loudly rang out.

"He's here! He'll burn me in hell! He'll drag me down with you! You selfish low life!" He began shivering up in what seemed to be a pathetic attempt to comfort himself. Tears poured from his red rimmed eyes. His whole body started to violently shiver like a leaf on a windy day. His face went stone cold momentarily leaving him with no emotion. All at once, his face twisted into a deep anger while his bony hands reached out towards me. Ezekial's frail body lunged forward.

His frigid fingers wrapped loosely around my small throat finger by finger. Ezekial's quick lunge toppled the chair that held my weight. My neck collided with the cold tiled floor. His knees straddling my stomach tightened while the worker ran over with sedative in hand to calm the raging man. The low dosage failed causing the worker to drop the needle. He grabbed for Ezekial, trying to pull his weight off of me while the unhinged sickly man yelled into my face, droplets of his saliva falling to my skin. "Go through!", he screamed with an urgence repeatedly. A subtle move from his pocket to my hand allowed for a crumpled piece of paper to be transferred to my palm. Finally, the worker found success in removing Ezekial and dragging him away.

Stress and exhaustion flowed through my body daring to explode as I looked into the mirror that hung on my wall. A splotchy redness remained on my neck from his fingers. Unwrapping the wrinkled paper, a cross was drawn with a small circle on the left bottom, and a large circle on the right top. Each circle laid slightly above or below the cross.

Since Ezekial was my last patient of the day, I packed my things and went home for the night. On the car ride home, I turned on the radio. I kept fumbling with the paper in my right hand. Hopefully the tune of music could alleviate the emotions that were exuding from me. However, those hopes were quickly taken as the radio irratically switched stations on its own. The music flipped between various hymns. The nun's voices loudly invaded my mind. I hated that type of music. No matter the reason, it filled me with a powerful anger. That was the last thing that I needed. My finger jabbed at the off button.

"Finally, peace and quiet." The words quietly left me under my breath. All of my attempts to relax on the way home failed. The atmosphere in the car felt so thick, and that smell. Did I leave food in the car? No, I wouldn't have. While I rolled down the car window a buzzing sound accompanied it. I couldn't quite put my finger on it but something felt so different. The air was so thick I almost couldn't breathe, and my chest felt so heavy like someone put a weight on it. It felt like something was burning holes into the back of my head with their eyes. All of it was excruciatingly unwelcoming. I'm just tired. Ezekial's actions are getting to me.

"Julia", a little boy's hoarse whisper filled the air. Half way through my name, the voice was no longer of a boy but was replaced by a man's hoarse voice.

I could feel the words being breathed out on the back of my neck. The warm breath fell on my skin just as clearly as the words filled my ears. The hymns started playing again. The volume increasing with each passing second. My eyes flicked to the rear view mirror. A large smokey black figure sat staring back at me. It's rows of serrated pearly white teeth flared out while his head shot backwards, his skull touching his back and lunged at me. My harsh slam on the brakes caused the car tires to screech in protest on the paved road. I swung the door open and grabbed my phone to call

911. After frantically getting out of the car and calling the police my eyes darted back and forth trying to spot the perpetrator.

"911 What's your emergency?"

"I - I think" In such a pressing time I couldn't find the words. They were there, fighting to get out. I couldn't formulate the words because although I know what just happened to me, there was nothing there.

"I'm sorry, I called on accident"

"Ma'am are you sure?"

"Yeah, I'm sure"

"Okay, thank you for letting me know"

The line went dead. My eyes brimmed with tears. I'm going insane. At this rate I'll end up losing my mind. Maybe, I'm just like some of my patients. No, I just need sleep. After collecting my thoughts, I went back into my car. I need more sleep.

Soon, my car reached a rolling stop in the driveway. Gravel crunched under the car tires, a familiar sound that was comforting, signaling my arrival at home. I stood in front of my dark purple and black painted Victorian style house. Hesitantly, I walked inside and flipped the lights on to the kitchen. The wine red walls soothed my anxiety. After pouring a glass of water, I went to my bedroom. Grabbing the melatonin from my nightstand drawer and swallowing it, I layed down allowing my body to sink into the soft mattress and ease into the comfort of the blackness that pushed me to sleep.

"Julia! Julia, I found you. Don't you recognize me?"

"Come out from the corner please. I want to look at you." His voice was small and boyish. The tiny figured boy concealed everything about him except his height within the poorly lit corner of my room.

"You didn't want to look at me a while ago. In fact, you refused. I think that you didn't want me. I loved you so much and you let me die, they burned me alive and you did nothing. What was it about me that you didn't like?"

"Come out from the dark and talk to me. Come here to me." His foot began to take a step out of the dark corner, and into the dim moonlight.

His voice boomed and deepened, his body stretched and his head reached the ceiling. His bones snapped and popped at his growth while they tore out of his stretching skin. When the figure stopped growing, new skin grew on him creating a sizzling sound while it bubbled. His skin was burned as if someone threw acid on him. Long, sharp white nails grew from his burnt calloused fingers. His teeth were absent from his mouth while he slyly smiled, and his eye sockets were hollowed, pouring a dark threatening red. His voice deep and angry, "YOU PUT ME IN THE DARK! YOU DID THIS TO ME!" His hesitant steps became a quick and impatient run.

My body rushed with an intense fear as I jerked up from the bed, balling my dark blue sheets tightly in my fist. A shooting pain went through my chest, most likely by the fault of my heart threatening to explode from out of it. The sound of splattering rain hitting against the window drummed in the background. Although I was awake, fear still held me captive. Something still felt off. Not the type of uneasy feeling a child gets after a bad dream. Instead, a feeling as though I was just sentenced to death. I held my breath, catching something out of the corner of my eye. Slowly, my head turned to examine what might be there. After finding nothing, the basic human instinct kicked in to breathe. A loud thunderous boom cracked through the sky, shaking the house followed by a bolt of lightning that creeped it's way inside shedding light by the open curtain.

Slowly creaking open, my old wooden door invited drafts of cold air to slip into the bedroom biting at my skin. The only thing in my sight was the pitch blackness that filled the space in front of my room until another bolt of lightning struck in the sky. I quickly turned to my side, and flipped the lamp on. At the end of the hallway, a small figure appeared. Seemingly the same height from my nightmare. Another boom of thunder caused a vibration to set out through the house's walls. A giggle echoed throughout the house.

Adrenaline took over and induced me to jump out of bed running towards the threshold of my door, yet not leaving and stepping into the hallway. Needing to know who was there, I flipped the hallway light on. A small boy in blue jeans, and a white sweater with black shoes came to light.

"Hello?" The words sounded unsure as they fell out of my mouth. Slowly raising his hand, his finger fell over his red lips. A crash of thunder broke out. The mass vibration caused a glass frame to fall from the hallway wall and shatter into hundreds of pieces as the wooden frame fell gracelessly onto the ground.

"Shhh, if he hears you, he'll find you" He looked to his left, tilting his head up at an odd angle, which was a short hallway that led to a sitting room. A low whistle erupted and a tall shadow appeared on the right wall of the hallway. Terror filled the little boy's face as he ran towards my room. His small feet clicked against the wooden floor. Again, lightning bolted in the sky followed by thunder that dared to cause another vibration in the structure of the house. Time slowed, while the rain hit the window, the man's low whistle bounced off the walls, and the clicking of the boy's shoes echoed away.

CHAPTER TWO

PROVING YOU

T HE LIGHT OF THE HALLWAY flickered once, again, and then one
last time before it went out completely. Loud, pounding footsteps
followed in suit to the boy's. Not a single thought traced my mind while I
watched the events being unfolded. Without me thinking, my hand began
to push on the door. Perhaps I should close it now, or do I wait for the boy?
A boy that had never met my acquaintance. Despite the roaring fear that ran
through my veins, I couldn't let an innocent child get hurt and do nothing.

"WAIT!" The little boy's frightened tone screamed out into the
blackness.

Closing my eyes, I gauged how close this small boy was to me. His small
but rushed steps sounded so close. At the same time, the man's heavy and
impatient steps sounded even closer. Although it was dark, I could see the
little boy's shaking figure in my room. He slammed my door shut. Sheer
terror motivated my body to push against the door, bracing for the impact of
whoever to be on the outside pushing back, trying to get in. Loud pounding
was coming from the opposite side. My ear drums felt as though they might
explode at any given second alongside my racing heart. Forceful blows began
to push the wooden door inward, daring to come off the hinges and relieve
itself of the mass stress that was being inflicted on it. With every breath

I've drawn on this earth the existence of God never particularly concerned me, until now.

"God I don't know if you're real but if you are then please help me and this boy now. Please save us. Please." Under my breath, I said the words with a heavy heart over and over hoping on a dime that maybe such a thing would be true.

All of the pounding ceased after a short moment of my "prayer". Both lights to the hallway and bedroom switched on again, giving a cheerful sign that maybe everything about this night was coming to an end. Looking at the bottom of the door, the gold hues of light caught my attention, allowing me to peer and see if anything might be lurking around. Thankfully, nothing remained.

After looking up, I saw the small boy shaking profusely. Since the man was nowhere to be seen or heard, I thought to wait it out a little before going to grab my phone in the kitchen. Curiosity began to replace my fear. Curiosity of this boy who mysteriously appeared flooded my mind. I kneeled down to his height and hugged his trembling body.

"I know you're scared right now, but I need you to tell me your name"

"I don't have a name. My mom didn't give me one"

What kind of mother doesn't give her child a name? Everyone has a name. Perhaps the fear that is causing him to shake is the exact thing that hinders him from saying much. As I held his hand, his grey eyes were overflowing with fear. How did he get in here? Every single door in this house was locked. He appeared too small to know how to break into a house, let alone bother to try. Chances are he was probably running from that man and saw my house. That's the most sensible answer. No, but not even such a sensible answer would explain how he got inside.

"Okay. How about I call you Atlas then. Is that alright?" Fear dispelled from him while he eagerly nodded his head. "Why are you here, Atlas?"

"I can't tell you. You wouldn't believe me. I think the bad man is gone now. What's your name?"

"Julia Hellan Bettington. How old are you, Atlas? Where are your parents?"

"My mommy left me 7 years ago. I don't know who my daddy is. I'm seven! Look at me! I'm really tall for a seven year old and I'm really strong, so strong! I think I look older than seven, unless I smile. My dimples make me look six."

Atlas let out a huge grin to prove his point. Regardless of the fact that children had never been something I welcomed or enjoyed the company of, admittedly, Atlas was adorable. The little guy's personality seemed especially clever and cute. Atlas's hair was deeply red with tight rounded curls. He didn't have any freckles but he had a small mole on his ear. His frame was small and although he didn't see it, he looked younger than seven. I pegged him to be five. As for his tallness, not a clue came to mind what he meant. His height allowed the assumption he was five. Although, now wasn't the time to tell him his appearance gave everything but maturity away.

"Atlas, I know you said that I wouldn't believe you regarding how you got into my home, but can you try telling me? I bet I'll believe you."

"Yeah I'll try. You might think I'm crazy" The boy bit his lip with anticipation.

If only he knew what type of people I deal with.

"Well, listen, someone sent me to watch over you because you needed protection from the bad man. I thought that you were in trouble and I didn't want him to hurt you! So, I came to protect you but the bad man is so big and scary that you ended up protecting me! I'm really sorry. I tried to help you but I'm just a kid. But listen! I'm gonna use my super strength and fight him! Look at these muscles!" He flexed his small arm trying to prove his point.

"Who sent you to protect me?" Surely no one would send a child in the line of fire.

"Mmm, that's a secret. I can't tell you that part." He looked away with reluctance.

"Atlas, stay here while I grab the phone to call the police." His small hand reached for my nightgown, tugging back.

"Don't! They won't believe you. They will think you're crazy! Listen, you can see me and the bad man because we want you to see us."

Standing up, I refused to accept such a philosophy. Atlas has been here far too long. Despite what he says there must be someone on this vast earth that takes care of him. Besides, the police need to catch whoever that guy was. I should stay at Salem's until they do. Gazing out of the window, contemplating what to do, I took note that the rain had calmed down tremendously and eased into a light peaceful drizzle.

Atlas tugged on the bottom of my red silk nightgown once again. His eyebrows knitted together and his chest started to heave up and down along with his eyes becoming glossy and teary. His gaze revealed a desperation that was escaping him. A frown etched onto his pale face when his tone changed from light and cheery to one of sorrow.

"Hey, trust me. I know I look small to you, but I can do a lot since I'm not like you. Since I'm good, I can act like a shield to stop the bad. You've never given me a chance. You don't understand! He'll get you if you don't get help! I'm trying to help you!"

"Atlas, what do you mean I'm not like you? Am I bad? It's not that I don't trust you. I just think that this is an adult situation that requires other people to help. What do you mean I've never given you a chance? You're just a kid. You shouldn't be involved in this type of stuff. You should be home." Frustration began to show on his face.

"I mean that I am not human! I'm a good spirit here to protect you from the bad spirit that is in your nightmares, in your home, and the one that keeps using me to make you vulnerable! He keeps acting like he is me just like he did in your nightmare and in the car! I can't tell you what I mean by saying you've never given me a chance. It's a secret." Atlas's eyes looked down to the floor.

"Listen kid, I don't know how you know about my nightmares or the car incident but you need to go home." What on earth is such a child thinking?

Possibly whatever situation he's in, he has created an alternate reality in order to cope with the pain that situation has produced.

"Oh you don't believe me then? Well watch this!"

Atlas's eyes filled with frustration while he balled up his small hands and pouted. In a single second, his body was nowhere to be seen. Confusion stopped me in my tracks while my eyes darted back and forth, all over the room trying to find the little boy who was so determined to protect me. My failed attempt to see this boy who disappeared out of thin air led me to a single conclusion that had been haunting me the past weeks. I must be going insane just like my patients. Collectively, my thoughts went into a frenzy thinking about daily life as a psych ward patient. Okay, I'm fine and so is everything else. All of this can be attributed to my lack of sleep. The correct course of action is to talk to a psychologist despite the crushing irony of me being one, take some meds, and time off of work, lots of relaxing and I should be fine. Unfortunately my mind and body is just in ruins currently. Nervously, I picked at my sore lips.

"Hey! I'm over here!"

Atlas's happy voice filled the house. Every bone in my body greatly urged me to ignore it all. This whole wretched day had been an extremely cruel fluke that took place due to a lack of self and is presenting itself, no, manifesting my mind into such a deformed state.

"Can you please come here? I think we should talk. You must be thinking you're crazy right now. Let me show you I'm good and real, okay?"

Alright, say I'm insane. If being crazy is my fate then it won't hurt to indulge in whatever this is for a little longer. At least, until I get help. I slowly exhaled and began taking cautionary steps towards Atlas, being careful to miss the small scattered pieces of shiny glass. Shakily exhaling, I ran my hand lightly against the soft white walls while taking comfort in the soft creaks of the wooden floor under my weight. Of all places, was it truly necessary to present himself at the end of the hallway where the man so openly was? That speaks volumes of being a trap. Say he was leading me to my possible death or a place I'd never be able to leave, all of this is simply the product of my delusion. It's not real, right?

"Okay Atlas, tell me why I'm not crazy when I'm talking to a boy who isn't real and hallucinating terrifying experiences. By all means, give me your best shot." Finally speaking to him my voice sounded less shaky than I thought it would be. I ran my fingers through my light brown hair as a source of comfort before I crossed my arms, hugging myself.

"You're funny, you know it?" His smile brightly reached his eyes, and his dimples made it impossible to not relax due to how adorable he was. Traces of anxiety slowly left me, clearing my mind. "Here is what's happening. I am real and I can prove it. OH! So is the man. You know how you prayed to God and the bad man went away?"

"Yes, but I don't see how that connects. Oh wait, you said you were a good spirit, right?" The doubt continued to stand strong within my mind.

"God gave me permission for me to help you. With the deal I made, He can only help sometimes. I asked Him for help back there. Since God is the most good and powerful, He kicked that bad man out! Plus if you still don't think I'm real then you can invite a friend over, and I'll drop something, and your friend will see it too! If more than one person sees the same thing then don't you humans think that it's real?"

"Okay, once my friend, Salem, arrives you can do whatever you may. Hey kid, if you want two people to see the same thing then why don't you show yourself to her as well?" He smiled and shook his head as though the answer had been spelled out to me in bold letters.

"It doesn't work that way. I'm here to protect you, not Salem. Also, that would require a lot of explaining, and I have to stay busy protecting you. I have rules to follow. I can't just show myself to the world."

After I studied Atlas more, the realization struck me like a freight train. The reminder of a person who you wish to forget most is a very painful thing. Reflexively my neutral facial expression fell into a frown as the memories played back in my mind, threatening to consume me all at once if I didn't reel myself back to reality.

"What's wrong?" Atlas's voice rang in my head snapping me away from my thoughts, grounding me back to reality.

"Your hair, it's the same as my mother's." So many of his physical attributes reminded me of people that I tried so hard to forget.

Atlas tightly hugged my legs.

"I'm sorry if I make you sad. I always seem to do that." His voice sounded like he had a hole in his heart, desperately wishing for it to be filled.

The second I stooped down to his height, I embraced him in hopes that his sad eyes would return to his normal cheerful state. How do you comfort a depressed kid? Did I truly refer to this hallucination as a genuine child? Or is he real? He is right about the God thing... No, I'm not making any final decisions until Salem comes over tomorrow. Whether or not she sees what he does will be the deciding factor.

"No, Atlas you didn't make me sad. Why don't we play your favorite game?" Even though Atlas may be a hallucination, the thoughts dancing around in my head of the kid being real is all the more welcomed than the alternative.

"I want to play tag!" Atlas jumped up, creating a creak in the floorboard, excitement filling his voice.

"Okay, I'll give you a ten second head start. No going in the basement, got it?" At least, he didn't say hide and seek. I've seen enough horror movies to know what happens when you play hide and seek with a ghost child. Atas giggled while he hurriedly ran off alternating with the occasional skipping. Soon enough the creaking stopped from the floorboards after he jumped onto the soft brown rug, cushioning any sound that may arise from the weight of his feet. His giggle was filled with innocence, making it impossible to not find cute. With each passing second, the thought of him being real held more appeal. We played several rounds of tag.

"Alright, that's enough." I could barely speak for panting from exertion. Yes, I was out of shape, but Atlas was also incredibly fast.

"Can we please play one more time? Please! You'll be my favorite person to ever walk this earth!" His eager eyes and clever smile with dimples showed that Atlas thought he could win me over.

Ruffling his hair, I thought about continuing such a tiring game. "Atlas, we played tag for an hour. I'm not a ghost so I get tired. Besides, I have work tomorrow. I can't stay up all night. Speaking of which, do you need a place to sleep or do ghosts not sleep?" He was so sweet and adorable, causing him to grow on me especially quickly. Real or not, he was funny and cute. After a moment of pondering, he looked around and squinted his eyes before giving an answer in a defeated tone.

"I don't need to sleep, but I can if I want to. It gets really boring sometimes so I end up sleeping a lot. Lately though, the bad man has been scaring me so I just don't sleep since I'm all alone." Atlas's fearful eyes looked down to the floor as he shifted his weight to the opposite foot and solemnly played with his small fingers. Holding back what seemed like a crashing wave of emotions, he hid behind those fearful grey eyes reluctant to reveal the impact of the crashing waves.

"Atlas, do you want to sleep in my house? You can sleep on the couch near my bed." His fidgeting fingers stopped, and a wide smile revealed his dimples on his face, leaving nothing but happiness to show the outside world. Leading him up to my room, grabbing a fluffy white blanket, I tucked him in on the grey couch that was to the right of the bed.

"Goodnight." Atlas flashed a warming smile before I went off to bed.

"Goodnight" He said the word with ease as he closed his eyes, snuggling up to the warm blanket.

Although last night was quite peculiar, I decided to maintain my normal routine the next morning. Waking up, I prepared for yet another long day of work that would hopefully be better than the last. Before I went off, Atlas sat on the red rug watching cartoons despite the availability of a couch that wasn't but three feet away from him. Salem looked at me with grave accusation while I clocked in.

"Where is my ramen? I left it here. Did you eat it?" Her tone was sharp, leaving no room for argument. Once she made up her mind, nothing could change it even if all the necessary evidence was carefully presented out to her. Such a trivial thing to allow one's self to be engulfed by. Fumes of anger were coming off of her, while we stood in the white painted room of the psych hospital.

"Salem, if I had time to steal someone's ramen, I would use it to sleep." She glared at me, daggers ready to throw through her accusing eyes. If looks could kill, my heart would no longer be beating. "Hey, you should come over tonight. We can finally catch up."

"Yeah sure, but I can't stay out for that long. Anyway, Herrison decided to use his crap as paint on the walls. I have to go clean it up. By the way, I know you ate my ramen. Buy me a new one." Her eyes rolled as she walked through large double brown doors, bracing herself for crap clean up duty.

"Oh, aren't you just the sweetest of the bunch?" Sarcastically, the annoyed words left my lips just as the doors were closing.

Gratitude resided in my heart when I thought about how, unlike Salem's damned soul, cleaning up human feces is not required of me. A small chuckle escaped me while I listened to my pale pink heels clicking against the tile grey floor. Somehow, despite the events that unfolded last night I feel more free than I have in so many years. Usually, the utter and raw dread that would fill me when I headed to my office would be so painfully crippling. Today was different as I sat down in my black chair skimming over my patient's notes. Maybe it's the excitement to go home to something, rather than nothing.

Later, my boss, Mary, asked me to retrieve a green box to bring to her office. Usually as a psychologist, this wouldn't exactly be a task that I would do. However, she was in a rush, and I was not busy. Happily, I helped her out.

My shoes clicked against the grey tiling as I made my way to the storage room. I opened the door and switched the light on. The lights flicked, and began to buzz. A coat of thick dust covered the shelves, boxes, and everything else the room concealed. The unkempt state of the room showed the neglect of time. Particles of who only knows what slowly drifted down the air, only appearing in the streams of sunlight that the small window on the right wall permitted through. Boxes were carelessly stacked on shelves and there were stretchers, mannequins, and medical supplies everywhere. My attempts at rummaging through them all suddenly paid off.

"Yes! I found it!" Now that I think about it, why does the psych hospitals have mannequins? Forget it, I'll ask Mary later. As I made my way out the door something shiny caught my eye. Curiosity peaked within me as I walked over to the shining piece. Peculiarly, it was awkwardly stuffed into the corner, on the floor, next to the tall black shelves. Without a second thought my hand impatiently reached for the misplaced shiny object. My fingers only seconds away from grasping it, a strangled voice filled the surrounding air.

"One"

My blood ran cold at the sound invading my ears causing it to be difficult to summon the courage to turn around.

"Two"

Everything came to a crashing halt once my eyes laid upon the same figure's hollowed eyes bleeding red from my nightmares. His height soared ten feet tall with his bony back hunched over to fit in the room. Long, white, sharp three foot nails dangerously exuded from his burnt fingers. The same sly smile revealing the absence of teeth in his mouth. Not even his acid scorched skin nor his hollowed red bleeding eyes were different from that of my nightmare. Horror filled my face, revealing the terror that hardened my heart. Thoughts raced in my mind while I quickly calculated that the only way out was to run to the white door which he stood next to. My heart violently pounding, my palms sweating, my body filled with terror, I made a run for it.

"Three" His sly smile grew wider appearing to have joy in playing cat and mouse with me.

Reaching for the door, I placed my hand on the golden knob ensuring to have a tight grip. Happiness flickered in me like a candle before it's blown out.

"Got you!" His laugh boomed in the room filling my head, and the lights flickered with a buzz. Any trace of happiness left me the moment his long burnt fingers carefully wrapped around my ankle. Yanking my body to the cold tile floor, he dragged me towards him. My nails frantically clawed at the floor trying to escape. While he dragged me, his nails pierced my skin only for him to dig them deeper, practically clawing into my flesh. They tore violently through my soft flesh, slicing layers of skin. A thick stream of warm blood quickly ran down my leg. My scream filled the air as he used his other hand to slam the door shut. Pulling me over to him, he pressed his hand harshly against my mouth as to muffle my pained scream. Hot tears trickled down the side of my face, falling to the floor. Each long second grew into an agonizing eternity. Helplessness crushed my aching soul. All of my attempts to escape were futile under his binding hold. Bringing his head down to mine, the blood from his eye sockets dripped onto my cheek. The cold liquid traced down to the floor.

"One more tormented soul dragged down to hell. Do you feel life fleeting from you, Julia?"

He stuck his nails deeper into my leg and then pulled out. Dark red covered his once white nails and dripped down his elbow. Darkness began to take over in place of my fleeting vision. I had no more hope left in my soul. Between the loss of blood, excruciating pain, and raw terror my body seemed to be giving up on me.

Chapter Three

Breathing Again

Atlas's Point of View

"Julia! Julia wake up!" Her face was unhealthily pale and strained. I must have come too late and now the bad man got her. I tried so fast to get here! My powers sensed she was in trouble. By the time I walked in, the bad man was already laying over her and she had bled so much. No matter how much I shake her she won't wake up! The only way I can help is by finding a human and leading them here.

As I walked around the psych hospital I met some pretty scary people. If only I could show myself. Rules are rules though. What am I supposed to do about this?! How has no one gone looking for Julia yet?! Eventually I found a girl with brown hair and eyes. She was short and walked weird. Maybe she had a limp. Her name tag read Mary in yellow letters. She was sitting in the break room all lonely like with her head buried in her hands. I think if I open the door to this room then she might go investigate and I can open the door in the hallway that leads to where Julia is!

"Alright, let me just push this one open." I made sure to push the white door hard enough for her to notice but not too hard or else it would startle her.

Mary asked if anyone was there and began walking towards the door. I quickly ran to the door in the hallway and opened that one. She followed into the room. Right before she was about to walk in her face went pale white.

"Oh my gosh Julia!" She said in disbelief. She then turned around and ran away towards the medic room. Her shoes pounded against the floor. I watched as she frantically explained the situation to a man in a white coat. He looked quite funny because he was bald. No, I have to focus. Julia was still breathing and her heart was beating. She is okay, right? I missed her so much over these years and I don't want to lose her again. She is probably just taking a rest. Humans do that, no it's the body that does that when it needs to heal.

The Mary lady came rushing back along with the bald man. They both looked concerned. The bald man picked her up, took her to the room, and looked at her carefully. Julia opened her eyes up slowly. Mary grabbed her by the shoulders, crinkling Julia's brown shirt.

"Julia, are you alright? I'm so sorry. This is all my fault."

The doctor then said "Your wounds aren't terribly severe. Your artery was barely missed. The wounds weren't deep enough that you needed to be sent to a real hospital. I stitched them up but you really shouldn't be walking too much on it since there are so many of them."

Julia slowly looked over to me. Her eyes went wide. Is she scared of me? No, maybe she is just surprised to see me over here. I hope she doesn't start talking to me. They will think she is crazy if she does. I'll smile at her to let her know that it's okay.

"Mary, what do you mean it's your fault?"

"It's just that I know I should have fired my nephew after he accidentally let one of the patients escape. He's done it again and you suffered the consequences. I could have sworn I saw you in your office when I was checking to see if everyone was okay after we got hold of the patient, but apparently I was terribly mistaken. I'm so sorry. I had him fired just a little bit ago. I just didn't fire him the first time because I thought that he deserved another chance and I was sadly wrong. Please forgive me, Julia!" Mary's face pleaded for forgiveness and looked guilty.

"Of course, Mary, I know you're not at fault. Your nephew's mistakes aren't your own. Don't blame yourself, okay?" For a second I was surprised by Julia's words. No, Mary is most certainly at fault for this, Julia.

"Alright, I'll help you out to your car."

As Mary helped Julia get into the car she motioned her head for me to get in. For a second, I thought she didn't want to see me again, but I was wrong. I would have been sad if she didn't want me anymore. I got in the back seat and debated if I should put a seatbelt on. I know I'm not human but I sure wouldn't mind acting like one for a bit. I mean goodness me, yesterday I even played tag, got to sleep, and was tucked in like a real kid!

"Atlas, are you alright?"

"Hm? Oh yeah, I'm okay, just thinking is all. I'm sorry that I couldn't get to you in time. The building was too big. I couldn't find you at first. You're going to be okay though, right?"

"Yeah, I'll just need a little bit of time to heal so don't blame yourself. I know that you said you needed to protect me, but you don't always have to put yourself in danger. It's not safe for you."

"It's not safe? What am I going to do, die?" She glared at me through the rearview mirror. It's true, I've already died. I let out a laugh and shook my head.

"Regardless, I hope you understand my point. I don't know what you did before you came into my life but while you are here, just be a kid. You may be a ghost but I see how scared you get when things like this happen. You should still take care of yourself."

"Oh" My voice was void of any emotion.

I know that "Oh" is a very small response to what she said but that's a lot to think about at my age. Except for the part where she said "I don't know what you did before you came into my life". I've always been around. I just wish she and I could have talked sooner. I wish she could have seen me sooner. Now I'm just sad. I should see if Julia wants to play a game when we get home. That would cheer me up. What games can we play without having her move? Is there such a game?

"Julia, can we play a game when we get home?"

"How about Uno, love?" She smiled brightly. Julia must like Uno then. I've never played but it sounds fun. I smiled revealing my dimples. She called me love. Does that mean she's accepted me?

"Only if you teach me how to play." She nodded her head.

We arrived home and after multiple defeats and wins in the game of Uno, Salem arrived in her purple car. Her bright headlights blinded me for a second. Purple is quite a weird color for a car. Whatever floats your boat, I guess. She walked in and immediately started asking about the incident earlier today. I have to say that the man escaping today was perfect timing. If that didn't happen then how in the world would Julia explain herself?

After I was bored listening to their conversations, I decided to show her that I am real and not some hallucination. What should I start with? I'll knock that elephant toy off the table. Darn it! Salem didn't notice. Would Julia get angry with me if I pushed something breakable? It is for a greater cause so it should be fine. That blue flowered glass vase looks perfect.

"Listen vase, it's for a greater cause. You're pretty but I have to sacrifice you so I can get Julia to understand that she isn't crazy. I hope you've lived a good life." Just a little farther, one more push. After the vase made quite the crash Salem and Julia jumped and looked over to the source. Oops, maybe that was a mistake. Can I smile my way out of trouble?

"Did you leave it on the edge?" Salem continued to stare at the broken pieces on the wooden floor.

"Huh, I guess so. I'll clean it up now. Continue with your story, Salem."

I guess Julia isn't angry because she smirked after Salem mentioned something about it and then let out a sigh of relief. She gave me a smile while she was cleaning the vase up and whispered "One more time". I then decided to target the glass that Salem was drinking out of. Julia didn't seem too happy as I pushed the glass of water over causing it to overflow onto the floor. It's not that she looked angry about it but not happy. Her eyebrows furrowed and a slight frown showed on her face. Let me switch it up. It's best not to break or spill anything now. Next I banged on the wall and Salem seemed to be weirded out. After that, she said her goodbyes to Julia and said "Fix your house, will you?".

"I told you I'm real!" Since Salem couldn't hear me I let it out. Julia then waited until the door was closed to answer.

"Thankfully, how about we get some sleep? I'm really tired."

I didn't want to sleep but it looked like she was so tired. I thought it was better not to fight it. I was surprised when Julia tucked me in again and told me good night. I expected her to just go to sleep. Well, I'll close my eyes and try to sleep I guess.

JULIA'S POINT OF VIEW

The sunlight poured through the side of my tan curtains, abruptly ending my sleep. My alarm went off only a couple of minutes after the rude interruption. Usually, I would be reluctant and lay in bed a couple more minutes just to buy myself some more time before the poor reality of work truly set in. However, due to Mary feeling bad and giving me time off, I decided to lay in bed for 20 minutes. I wasn't avoiding anything today, I just wanted to relish in the comfort of the warm blankets.

"Juliaaaa," Atlas decided to draw out the a for whatever reason. His tone was light and filled with joy. Does he need food? No, I wouldn't think so.

"Yes, Atlas?" The grogginess in my voice caused me to internally cringe. Such a sound was painful to hear, even if it was my own voice. For the first time in years the chance to sleep longer danced before me. All I needed to do was seize it. The sleepiness caused me to turn away from Atlas and nuzzle my face into the pillow, hoping he would pick up the signal that I longed for more sleep.

"I'm hungry. Can you make me some food?" Now that question caught me by surprise. Turning over back to him and opening my eyes I asked the question that came to mind.

"A ghost, needing food?"

"Okay, you got me. I just wanted to taste some food, ya know? I'm not hungry but I would sure like to eat anyway." Smiling warmly, he revealed his dimples while his grey eyes danced with excitement.

"Alright, give me a second." How could I deny such a cheerful boy something so simple?

Atlas's feet could be heard speedily running down the stairs with an impatience that reminded me of a child on Christmas Day. The thought of making a ghost some food truly amazed me. Rubbing my eyes, I practically rolled out of the comfort of my warm, cozy covers causing a thump on the floorboards. I would prefer to make my usual eggs with mushrooms for breakfast, but I don't know what he would like. I looked over to him sitting on the rustic wooden chair pushed up to the dining room table, smiling brightly and holding a silver fork in his hand. With every move I made, his eyes followed me with patience.

"What would you like to eat? I usually do eggs with mushrooms."

"That sounds so good. I love mushrooms. Can you please make the eggs scrambled?" Atlas's eyes squinted questionly while his voice heightened with uncertainty near the end of his sentence.

I nodded my head at this. Scrambled eggs had always been a personal favorite of mine. If eggs were ever to be eaten by me, then they had to be scrambled. As for the mushrooms, what's not to like about them? Cracking the eggs on the side of the black pan, I whisked them in a bowl and sliced the mushrooms, throwing them in. After cooking, I sat down at the table with Atlas. He looked so content with eating something so simple. His parents that abandoned him truly missed out Not only is he cute, but he is incredibly caring. He's generally polite as well. Not to mention he is incredibly brave, always putting others before himself. What type of kid jumps into the line of fire for someone who he doesn't know?

"Atlas, what is the thing that keeps trying to get me?" Slowly looking up the kid placed his fork down on the glass plate causing a clatter sound to follow in suit.

"Oh, the bad man is a demon. I think he wants your soul. I heard they don't stop until they get what they want but between you and me, we can beat him." Atlas gave me a thumbs up, resuming to eating the warm food.

"Isn't that comforting. So what do we do to stop him?" Once again, placing his fork down, he waited until he finished chewing to answer.

"Do you believe in God?" He raised his right eyebrow alone.

"I think so after what has happened with you and the demon."

"You should start reading the Bible. It'll help strengthen your will and soul. You should also start praying. Evil spirits cower in front of God. They don't like Him. If you don't want to be religious, then that's okay. That's why I'm here. God never forces humans to have a relationship with Him. They cower in front of me too. It'll just take longer." After smiling, he continued eating.

"Huh." Was all I could get out as I pushed the cold eggs around on my glass plate occasionally causing the fork to scrape against it.

So, I have a choice if I'm religious then. Atlas looked like he didn't have a care in the world as he was finishing up his food. After he was done, he had a very determined look on his face. I've never seen him so serious, eyebrows furrowed, not a smile nor frown on his face, and quizzical eyes.

"We should play some tag." His tone was flat and no nonsense.

"Okay Atlas, we can't play tag. I don't feel like running on my leg." A chuckle left me. That was what he wished to say?

"Sorry, I forgot. We could play hide and seek?" Atlas's eyes were filled with such hope that saying no wasn't in me.

"I'll count to thirty." My tone was light in an attempt to match the bubbliness that he portrayed.

Hide and seek seemed like a better option. If I am being honest here, there aren't a whole lot of games that I really am physically up to. In fact, there will probably be only a couple rounds played. Next, would be a board game, television, more food, a story, and then lovely sleep. Somehow the nightmares didn't affect my overwhelming urge to sleep.

I yelled the classic "Ready or not here I come!". Searching top to bottom in the house, I failed to locate Atlas. Could he be switching places? If so, then he is cheating. A light giggle erupted behind me. I turned around to go catch him but instead I only saw his foot as he was running around a corner. He let out another giggle except this one was a bit lower than the last causing suspicion to rise up in me. Shaking my head, I buried any suspicion, chalking it up to the fact that everything left me on edge recently. Chances are I am reading too much into it.

"I'm going to get you!"

Just as I rounded the corner I saw his back going down into the basement. Momentarily, I stopped. I didn't hear the sound of the basement door opening. Cautiously going down, I leaned on the wall next to me. The once white color was turned into a hue of yellow over time. Through my shirt I could feel the small bumps on the wall that had made their home there long before I moved in. Victorian style home's basements always had an extra creepy layout. The memory of me telling him not to go in there played in my mind like loud music. The kid's giggles bounced off the concrete wall traveling to the staircase, invading my ears.

"Atlas, I told you not to go in the basement. If you can't follow the rules, then we can't play games. Come out from wherever you are and let's go back upstairs." In order to convey seriousness, I used an authoritative tone.

Never in my life was it necessary for me to be stern with a child, but this time I had to. You let a kid break one rule then he slowly pushes until he breaks another and another. Before you know it, he is calling all the shots. Ghost or not, rules are rules when you're living with someone. I saw him hiding under an old antique table that was in a room hidden from plain sight. You had to crawl into it since there was a heavy metal door halfway off its hinges. I made my way into the room. Dust and dirt thickly coated my palms while my jeans rubbed against the hard, cold concrete floor. Standing up after I brushed my knees, I put my hand assertively on my hip. Waving my hand, I motioned for him to come out.

"Atlas, come on. It's dangerous here. Let's go."

He stayed crouched under the table. Determination set in his eyes that his will to leave was close to none. Walking over, I waved at him to come out while I raised both my eyebrows. He propped up his elbow on his leg and with a single finger motioned me to come closer. A smirk slowly played on his face as he cocked his head to the side. An uneasiness arose within me as I inched ever so closer to him. The sound of my feet shuffling against the thick dust coated floor echoed in the small room. He wiped the smirk off his face, fully smiling at me by the time I crouched down to his level, becoming closer to him. Right as I opened my mouth to say something, Atlas vanished from thin air. Annoyance grew inside of me but I thought it better to simply walk away, and stop playing rather than lose my temper.

I crawled back out of the room and began my walk upstairs. With my first step, barely landing my feet, his giggle echoed. Momentarily pausing I shook my head to myself and decided to continue up. With my next step, a loud boom erupted behind me as though someone dropped something of incredible weight. Jumping at the sound, I harshly bit my lip in fear, feeling my heart pick up pace. Hesitantly turning my head, I looked at Atlas behind me. Hints of red took over the color of his eyes. His nostrils flared giving off the impression that rage was rising within him. My stomach sank as I realized that it wasn't Atlas at all, rather a malicious evil. After gathering myself, I turned around to go up the stairs.

"Wait!" The demon's strangled voice angirly screamed loudly. So loud that my hands quickly covered up my ears, stopping me in place. Only after a few seconds did my body find itself capable of moving.

Loud footsteps ran after me. With each step, they pounded louder and came more and more quickly. Every step sounded like a sledgehammer banging against a wall. Fear caused my heart to pound violently and filled my head with thoughts of painfully dying. Right when the steps came close behind me, they stopped abruptly. Nervously, I looked behind only to find no one there. Adrenaline aided me while I rushed up the stairwell. My gaze stayed glued on the light from upstairs, thinking that all I needed was to reach it in order to obtain safety. At the threshold, the demon's bleeding eyes met mine. He let out a demonic growl once he shoved my body down the stairs. A small scream escaped my lips.

Tumbling down the bottom of the stairs, my body continued to roll and smack harshly against the brick wall. With the wind knocked out of me, I hoarsely coughed and gasped for air trying to relieve my aching lungs. All the things in my line of vision became fuzzy. Blinking my eyes, I looked up, hoping to find the demon absent from my view. To my relief he was gone. I began to try to get up, but the excruciating pain prohibited me from graduating onto my legs. I collapsed from under my hands and knees, practically wheezing. The light to the basement flickered with a static noise daring to give up despite being such a pressing time.

"Julia!"

Atlas's concerned voice filled the space between us. As he stood on the top of the dusty wooden stairs, I could only think of my conflicting feelings. On one hand, I greatly appreciated his helping gesture concerning my state. On the other hand anxiety filled me thinking of him getting hurt. The anxiousness outweighed the appreciation, and I only wished for him to stay out of the cross fire. Atlas ran down the stairs, but once he got near me the lights flickering came to a halting stop. Atlas's concerned self grabbed my arm trying to help me up just as the demon appeared again. He drew up his long burnt arm and sent Atlas flying across the room. His small body collided into the wall creating an umph sound, as he slowly slumped down. Fear ran through my blood as the acid burned demon hunched over the poor boy.

Chapter Four
Fearful Fighting

I BEGAN TO GET UP, PUSHING through the pain that plagued my body. Worry killed me from the inside while Atlas's body laid hunched over and unconscious on the dusty floor. The heaving demon mockingly traced his nails over Atlas's face. He stretched his fingers wide around the child's head with his palms against Atlas's cheek. The demon's thumbs free, he centered them with Atls's eyes while he moved his nails to puncture them. I painfully limped my way behind the hunched over being. The demon breathed so heavily, as if he was always struggling to retain air in his lungs. Up close I could see boil and blisters on his skin. Runny yellow liquid oozed like a river out of them.

In the same second, the demon acknowledged my presence. He took a step towards me. His figure loomed greatly. Even though his eyes were hollowed, they held such hatred. He put his head down towards mine, straining to speak. The demon's hot breath fell on my face. With each sentence he spoke he took a step towards me, and I one back.

"Do you see my eyeless face bleeding red? I'll do the same to you, except it won't just be your eyes I'll take. I'll pull your eyes out of your head and laugh as they bleed and your screams fill my ears, only that will be last so you can watch as I mercilessly take everything else from you. One by one,

I'll take your friends until loneliness fills your heart. Next will be your limbs, as I slowly tear them from your body, ensuring that you don't die until I take your eyes and then rip your heart from your chest. I'll bathe in your guilty blood. The hounds will eat your limbs delightfully stretching your skin until it rips off. Over time, I'll take your soul so you'll be weak and restless in your last days. I'll make sure you'll beg for your own death out of misery and pure pain, Julia Hellan Bettington. One more tormented soul, dragged down to hell. You'll be my mouse in the trap. Every anguished squeal will be music to my ears. Every twitch of your limbs shall be to my everlasting amusement."

By the time his harsh words were spoken he had me pressed up against the wall. He brought up his arm and began to point his sharp nails towards my stomach. I held my breath in anticipation for them to pierce my skin. Just as he began to apply enough pressure to make me bleed, Atlas picked up an old wooden board and hit the demon with such force that it flew clear across the room. Atlas was seeing red.

With great purpose and anger in his walk, he stomped over to the demon pathetically laying on the floor. Atlas had pulled a golden cross necklace out of his blue jean pocket and swung the chain around the demon's neck. The general area that the cross laid on his neck started to burn and the demon screeched and screamed so loudly that both the boy and I covered our ears. The noise was so intensely loud that the tables and chairs stored in the basement shook. Old glass vases shattered onto the floor. Suddenly, the demon had begun standing up violently clawing at his neck which made him bleed red. The demon seemingly disappeared from our eyes and presence, leaving us to pick up the aftermath. Where the demon stood the necklace laid with pieces of bubbling skin and blood surrounding it. I immediately ran to Atlas to see if he was okay.

"Do you still want me to stay out of the crossfire?" Atlas's tone was hard.

His eyes were filled with such a protectiveness that I needed a second before answering. Or rather, it was that I did not know how to address him with eyes so full of emotion. I desperately longed to express my growing gratitude towards him. However, I felt such frustration: Frustration to not be able to protect myself, frustration to not be able to protect him, and frustration for being in the situation. I was stunned because I had just witnessed such a drastic change in his character. Yet, under it all I felt relief. Relief that Atlas was here and okay, relief that I was saved.

"I think that if the situation calls for it, then I wouldn't mind your help. If it's something that I can do on my own though, then please allow me to. Thank you for saving me Atlas, truly."

Protectively wrapping my arms tightly around him, I gave Atlas a kiss on the cheek. For a moment, I kneeled there hugging him, relishing in the fact that he was okay. For whatever the reason, I quickly bonded with him and wished to protect him with all my might. His small hands hugged me back, letting me know that he was truly, in fact, well. After that, I grabbed his hand and walked upstairs only to realize that my stitches had opened and a lump had made itself a home on the back of my head. Blue and deep purple bruises covered my rib cage. Using a white towel, I applied pressure on my opened stitches. Getting them fixed was something that needed to happen. I'll just go to my work and get it done there. It'll be free and easy, no paperwork or waiting. Atlas looked at me expectantly as I turned to him.

"I'm going to go to my work and get my wounds stitched along with some ointment for my bruises. Would you like to go with me?"

Atlas weighed his options greatly before finally deciding. The small boy scrunched his eyebrows together, tapped on his chin with his pointer finger, scratched his head, and squinted his eyes before answering. Holding back a laugh, I wondered why he had to think so hard about a simple question.

"Yeah sure, I want to see the bald man again." Atlas's eyes filled with amusement as he smiled. He immediately teleported in the car and watched as I got in. He looked as though he was greatly pondering something.

"Do you think my mommy loved me?" His tone held a note of sadness while he peered up at me, seeming ashamed.

Flustered, and taken aback I was unsure how to answer the child. Perhaps my safest option would be to give him a reply that would answer him and close the topic.

"I'm sure your mom loved you very much. I'm sure both your parents did. Sometimes in life unexpected things can happen and we have to make very hard decisions to compensate. I think your mom abandoning you was one of those hard decisions."

"Why do you think she abandoned me? Was I not good enough for her?" His grey eyes held a knowing look as if he knew for a fact his parents didn't love him, more specifically his mother.

Oh, poor Atlas. A kid should never have to deal with these types of thoughts. Nonetheless, I'm positive my heart breaking from hearing this can't even begin to compare to the heartbreak he suffers. How to reply to him rendered me clueless. The only thing I can tell him is the truth. It's the only answer I have.

"Atlas, I know that this may not be the answer you're looking for, but it's the only one I can give you. So many people go throughout their lives without a care in the world. They don't care about who they hurt, or what consequences their actions have on others nor themselves. Everyone always runs into at least one person like that in their lives and most of the time they get impacted negatively because that other person is too self involved. Innocent people get hurt terribly by those types of people all the time. Like you, you were only a baby, Atlas. You were a baby and, for whatever reason, your mom left you. Your parents abandoned you because they are the type of people to not care how their actions affect others. As long as they get benefits from something, they'll cut down anyone in their path. You can't go back and change what was done to you. You can't. It's always going to be that way, that they abandoned you. So, you have choices to make. You can either choose to consistently ponder over what happened, ask why and then feel sorry for yourself, then let it eat you alive until you have nothing left, or you can accept what happened to you, and focus on the good. Focus on who you have now, and what you have now. You can look forward and keep going forward and fight to be better than what they did to you, and learn to love the life you have now. However, when you feel like you need to mourn the situation then do so, but don't do it constantly. Don't let it eat you. Don't let yourself have a pity party, and keep a normal routine. Don't let yourself mourn for more than two days. This world can be very cruel. Life doesn't allow you to mourn. It beats you until you're down, and unless you fight it and get back up no matter how much it hurts. Life will crush you without mercy and leave you bleeding to die. You'll become nothing then but a lump of anger, sadness, and self victimizing. You can choose that sad life or choose to be strong, optimistic, happy, and someone that adds a little more light into this world."

"I think that you just spoke a lot, like a whole lot. If we are being honest, it's the most I've ever heard you speak at once. It was actually good too, a little dark but I understand you have to get your little dark side in. Do you think I add a light to the world?" Curiosity was written all over his face, followed by a small smile.

"I think you shine brighter than a star, love." Atlas's small smile turned to a large grin that showed off his dimples and pearl white teeth.

Nothing like a car ride to provoke some deep thoughts. My answer seemed to soothe his soul. Speaking of soothing the soul, tea sounds wonderful right now. Very comforting in my opinion. It's warm, it's tasteful, relaxing, smells good, gives health benefits, and it has an abundance of flavors. Now I'm craving myself some nice herbal tea. I'll have to put the kettle on the stove when I get back.

"Atlas, how do you feel about having a warm cup of tea when we get back?"

"Is it anything like coffee? I do not like coffee. You see, coffee is just a bitter thing." Atlas's face held seriousness and what appeared to be a grudge as he crossed his arms and looked accusingly out the window.

"It's so much better than coffee." He was more than right about such a distasteful beverage.

"In that case, I would love some tea once we get back."

We arrived at the psych hospital and began the journey to the medical room. Eventually, we arrived and I explained the situation to the doctor. Of course, my failure to mention the whole demon part was imperative. Instead I told him that I tripped down the stairs while carrying a heavy dirty clothes basket down some very steep stairs. He, as per usual, did not seem to care about anything including how I opened my wounds. Maybe he just hates working here like me. In the midst of the awkward silence while he stitched me up, Atlas had a smirk on his face. No, it was more like he had a mischievous smile. Tapping the doctor on the shoulder, Atlas giggled into his hands when the doctor turned around to find nothing there.

I gave him a look that said quit it now, but he didn't make any attempt to look at my face. Probably because he knew if he did then he would have to stop. Surely he can feel the disapproval radiating off of me. Atlas proceeded to lightly blow on the back of his neck and the doctor swatted at the air. Atlas let out another joy filled giggle. However, I was not amused. Next, he decided it would be a grand idea to push the table where the doctor had his tools just far enough away that the doc wouldn't notice until he went to grab something. Of course, then he would only grab for his tools and proceed to grasp thin air trying to find it. Eventually the doctor looked up and sighed out of anger, then moved it back to it's rightful spot. This did produce a slight grin from me but I held back given that if the boy caught it, it would encourage him all the more. After he was done, I thanked him and began the journey back home.

"Julia, can we get a puppy?" Atlas's cheerful voice rang in my mind, pulling me away from my thoughts of tea.

"I don't think I have the time for a puppy. They are too much work." Puppies were difficult.

"Isn't hard work good though? Think about how cute it would be and how I could play with it all day, and how it could sleep with you when you have nightmares, or how it could become a guard dog. Let's not forget the fact that they are fluffy, and really just, think about the love they give."

"Think about how they pee and poop all over the floor because it isn't house trained. Think about all the training you have to do, and how annoying they can be. Don't forget the fact that they chew up things around the house and are way too full of energy. Oh, plus, they never want to stop playing. Under no circumstance will a puppy set a paw in our home."

"I have nothing to do while you are gone though. Julia, home is so big but it's only you and I that live there. Can't you open your heart just a little bit, like this much?"

He put his thumb and pointer finger close together with barely any space between. I do not like puppies. They are by far one of the most annoying things on this earth. No, kittens are so much worse. On the contrary, dogs are lovely. I wouldn't mind stopping by an animal shelter and getting a dog.

"How about this, I do not like puppies but we can get a dog that is no younger than three."

"YES! See Julia, look at the happiness you have given me. Soon, you will also get happiness from this. When that happens and the dog becomes a member of this family, I might just say I told you so." Atlas bounced with excitement under the buckle of his seat while he flashed a smile.

"We can go to a shelter in a couple of days and see if there are any dogs that we like."

The kid was right. I lived in a big house that's so empty and there is nothing for him to do there. Now I feel bad. He must get lonely and bored. I'm sure the dog will help, but I still want to do more for him. We should go get some toys. Toys, and then he can even pick his own bed sheets to use in the room next to mine.

CHAPTER FIVE

AN OWNER'S MARK

SOON WE ARRIVED HOME WALKING into the creaking brown door and closing it. Grabbing the blue and golden cast iron teapot, I put it on the low blue flames of the small stove. Waiting patiently next to the soothing sound of the bubbling water, I watched as the heavy steam found it's way through the spout. Grabbing two red mugs, I poured the hot water while a steamy cloud expelled from it. Carefully carrying them to the living room, I sat down on the inviting soft couch producing a humph from it. Wrapping my cold fingers around the warm mug I turned on the cartoon Tom and Jerry, the older version at least. I always preferred the version where they never talked. Salem disagrees greatly. Atlas appears to be enjoying it. After all of his smiles and laughs, he turned to me showing his dimples.

"Why don't they become friends?" His voice peaked with the utmost curiosity.

"Well, they are cat and mouse. You can't expect a cat not to try and get the mouse in his home. You also can't expect the mouse to let himself be caught. Besides, there wouldn't be a show if they were friends. There are a few episodes where they do team up. Only a few times though." Atlas solemnly nodded his head in agreement before he turned back to continue watching.

As soon as the show was over, we headed upstairs to go to bed. Pulling the fluffy white blanket over Atlas, I tucked him in and told him goodnight with a smile on my face. Going to my own bed, I nestled myself into the comfort of my warm heavy blankets, softly exhaling while the cushioned mattress conformed to my weight. Expecting to drift peacefully off into a heavy sleep, I was confronted with a million thoughts that left me wide awake. I began to think of the terrible mistake I made years ago as despair began to make a home in my heart. One decision shattered my heart, caused my whole world to fall in pieces, and resides constantly in the back of my mind. Recovery from it taunted me, dancing right in front of my fingertips, moving away every time I came closer. Why can't I change what happened? The two graves that I have dug gave me so much misery.

"Atlas, love, wake up" Lightly grabbing onto his shoulder I shook him slightly to rouse him awake.

An annoyed groan replaced any real response. Cringing on the inside, I remembered the promise Atlas and I had concerning getting him a dog. However, my eagerness to get the boy's toys and blankets of his own triumphed over my reluctance with the dog. The sunlight barely slipped through the side of the closed curtains allowing it to be dim inside the room but not bright nor dark. Understandably, it's six in the morning and that is outrageously early for a kid but he said it himself. He doesn't get tired. He just sleeps if he is bored. So, everything should be good and well.

"Atlas, if you don't get up then I'm sorry to inform you but we won't be able to get a dog, or toys for you. Not even bed sheets." My tone was playful, revealing my excitement. He sat up so quick that it made me jump a little. With a blink of an eye, the kid was up and ready to go.

"Toys? Bed sheets? Am I getting my own room?!" Atlas's dimpled smile warmed my heart. The joy that danced in his eyes made all my worries of getting the dog dissipate from me. Atlas's eyebrows were raised awaiting my reply. This single reaction suddenly made all of the hassle worth it.

"Yeah, you're right. It's a big house and it's just you and me. I was thinking that you fit in well here. So, it's only appropriate giving you the room nearest to mine. We can pick out a paint color, get some toys, decorations, make a theme, and get you some bedding. What do you think?"

"Oh my goodness Julia! You're the best ever! I can't believe you're getting me all that stuff! Let's go now!"

He seemed very happy with this proposition. Dimples surfaced on his face all the while the excitement bubbling up in him so much that it caused him to dance around, jumping with extreme enthusiasm. Ruffling his hair, I told him to give me a moment. After finishing my makeup, I walked out of my room. Across the hallway a door to another bedroom was cracked. A large figure loomed in the corner, barely visible. A deep incoherent whisper drifted out. Familiarity arose within me, but not the same kind previous to the demon. A disturbing sickness shot through my body, threatening to come out. Wesly?

I began to slowly walk forward, trying harder with each step to see what loomed in the dark shadows that belonged to the bedroom. Dragging my feet against the wooden floor, I choked on my fear. My shaky hands rested on the door. Hot tears stayed comfortably in my eyes. A whimper escaped me as my chest rose up and down close to hyperventilating. I began to gently push it open. Surely it can't be him. I'd never escape.

"Julia!"

Atlas's impatient voice sounded throughout the house. Looking over the polished stair railing, Atlas's joyful face flooded my vision. Once I glanced back, the unwelcomed looming figure in the dark shades of the room had willfully vanished. Crosses might just be what this house needs. During the allotted time that we are at the store, I'll pick some up.

Happily, I practically ran down the stairs, taking comfort in my own thumping footsteps. Leaving my house after seeing something like that seems unsettling. Quite honestly, all of this is unsettling except for Atlas. Surprisingly, despite the crushing evil, the kid makes up for it by a long shot with his goodness. Burying the incident that took place only moments ago I covered up all of my fear for Atlas. Such a wholesome child deserved all of the joys this day could possibly have to offer. Not an ounce of his remarkable bravery has gone unnoticed. Since my life isn't in immediate danger, I won't bother with it.

After we had gotten into the car and arrived at the store. We prepared to walk in. Before we did so it was imperative that I carefully explained to Atlas that while in the store and in the presence of others, I couldn't reply to him. The notion didn't appear to faze Atlas at all, nor his happiness. He picked out a dark blue bedding with planets all over it. Evidently they were especially dear and near to his pure heart. He then picked up dinosaur toys, trucks, cars, a whoopie cushion, swords, guns, and so much more. He even picked up big stickers of planets and stars to put on one of his walls. For Atlas's paint color he said that he wanted a lovely blue, nothing too dark, but most certainly nothing too light. He even picked out a couple of decent sized spaceships to hang on his ceiling.

Now, it was time to get the dog. By the time we got to the shelter Atlas ran into the old yellow painted brick building and began stopping by each dog's kennel. His small fingers poked through the chipped gray metal cages, stretching them as far as he could to pet their fluffy fur. Every time he did this I watched his facial expressions to see which ones he favored.

"Atlas, how come you keep stopping by and petting all of them?" My eyes gazed in curiosity at his gleeful face.

"I want to make sure all of them know what love feels like." His heart felt tone melted my own.

Now I thought that was very sweet. Atlas paying mind to each and every dog didn't bother me. We had so much time on our hands to utilize however we may please. Three kennels down, I saw an adorable black and grey Schnauzer mix. Immediately upon seeing the frightened thing, I rushed towards it. His body shook violently, signaling that fear filled his kind eyes.

"Atlas, how about this one?" The little child version of myself leaped with joy at my own words. The mixed dog seemed to love us both.

"Definitely this one." Stepping carefully into the cage with him, both of us pet him. He curled up to me and rested his head on Atlas's legs. As soon as he did this all shaking ceased in him. The storm that raged in his soft, shy brown eyes calmed to a sunny day.

Once we got home, Atlas and I began painting his room while we let the dog explore and get used to his new environment. The rich blue color added life and vibrancy to the room. Our wrists gently moved up and down as the bristles from the white paint brush quietly coated the wall in the new color. Chemicals from the paint entered into our airway causing a headache to myself, as Atlas was immune to getting sick in such worldly ways. The pressing headache was worth it given Atlas's dimpled smile. Within seven hours, including the breaks to play with the dog, we finished. Next on the agenda was drinking some tea and bonding with the dog until it was eleven. Atlas and I proceeded to happily walk up the stairs, readying our minds to power down and regain the energy that was lost.

Waking up to the sounds of the previous hymns from my car, I wiped the sleepiness from my eyes not yet fully grasping the gravity of the situation that was playing out before me. An annoying yet persistent tapping sounded throughout the room. It tapped in a slow rhythm as if to taunt me. Slow, yet softly it sounded. I squinted my eyes in a failed attempt to see around my bedroom. The only thing in sight was Atlas peacefully sleeping on the couch. Even then I could only see his silhouette and nothing more. That music though, I hate it. Ripping my thoughts away from the music, I pinched the front of my white cotton shirt and jerked my hand back and forth creating air flow. For whatever reason, it was extraordinarily hot. Sweat unforgivingly dripped from my warm forehead. Wiping it off with my hand, I grasped the blanket and removed it from my body. Putting all of my weight on my toes, I did my best to not wake the sleeping child. While my body woke up more and my senses became all the more keen it dawned on me that the hymns were undoubtedly coming from the lower level of the house.

I descended my way down the stairs, speeding up my pace in order to turn the hymns off. As I rounded the corner to the main sitting room, the brightness of the t.v. blinded my sleepy eyes. Various shades of color from it landed on the surrounding walls, allowing me some light in the darkness. The tapping continued in the mix of it all. Except now, the tapping was coming from all directions. When I reached the television that had the hymns playing on it, I hesitated to turn it off. For a brief moment I studied it. It was a video of a choir with children standing straight dressed up in a church. The hymns they sang were painful to my ears. I turned off the t.v. Blackness devoured any light that was given off from the television, temporarily blinding my once adjusted eyes.

The only noise that resounded throughout the house was that incessant tapping. Dragging my feet, I walked ever so closer to the basement door. Normally, I wouldn't go into the basement at such an hour, especially after what happened. In fact, I never really did go into the basement. Strangely, during this whole time I had felt so calm. Not a single ounce of fear ran through my blood. On the contrary, an increasing amount of annoyance ran through me. Anger filled me even more. Those two emotions bubbled up in me like a pot of tea left over the stove for too long.

My footsteps echoed in the basement. I flipped the light on once I reached the bottom step. The tapping was coming from the room that you had to crawl into. Wouldn't it be wise to turn back now? If I were to turn back would it even be of any matter? Regardless of what action I take, whatever is after me will get me when it so chooses. Surely there was a leak. Yes, such an excuse calmed the doubts that began to flood my mind like a broken dam. Once I examined the room, I saw that there was in fact a leak. Just like that, all of my doubts and fear that began to rise vanished as soon as they came. I'll have to call someone tomorrow. If only it could be fixed now. There is no way that I will be able to sleep with such a noise echoing from the basement, traveling its way up the stairs, and creeping into my room. Such a thing would invade my dreams, my head, no, my peace.

I turned around to leave. Long hairs on my head could be felt being manipulated as nails scrapped against my scalp, slicing open my skin just slightly. Warm blood trickled down the back of my head. Long, scorched fingers and nails gripped the right side of my face. A tight hold was cast and the left side of my head was slammed into the cold concrete wall. The pain was excruciating as I fell to the floor. My head grew lighter while warm blood trailed down my face. Though my brain screamed at my limbs to move; it cried that they couldn't.

Clawed hands tightly wound around my ankle. Shaky eyes prohibited my ability to clearly see. Sounds of my body shuffling against the floor with every pull of my ankle broke through the room. A stream of blood laid out where my head dragged against the cold floor. Feeling rather dazed, I attempted to call out for help. Every word came out as a toddler's mumble. Low, incoherent, and desperate, the mumbles fell on deaf ears. Under my delusional state, I could've sworn the feeling of heat coming closer to me as a long black hair slowly fell to the floor.

Chapter Six

Head Above Water

———◆◇◆———

"JULIA!? COME ON JULIA. I don't have all the time in the world to stay here. I have work you know? Not everyone is lucky enough to get attacked by a patient and then get a pity paid vacation by their boss. So come out, come out wherever you are."

Feeling like my brain was pressing against my skull and daring to explode was nauseating on all levels probable. Propping myself up on my elbows, the pain relentlessly became a million times worse than I thought was possible. Rubbing my temples, I feared that my brain would explode. The comfort of my blanket begged me to go back to the peaceful sleep that I was taken from. Dried blood resided on my pillow. When I brought my hesitant fingers up to the side of my head, I came into contact with a sticky substance. Pushing past the pain, I walked to the bathroom. Blurry vision caused me to stumble on my way. It only took one look in the mirror to see that on the right side of my head was deeply bruised and bloodied. In the meantime of me tracing back my steps in a sad attempt to figure out what happened to my head, I washed the blood off with a warm damp washcloth, ignoring the sting.

"Julia! How many times do I have to call out to you for you to show your face. My time is my money. You do realize the time, right? It's three. I'm on break so I have to get back soon. The fact that I have to come and find you when you invited me over here is kind of annoying."

"Can you shut up, Salem? I have a raging headache, and you're over here screaming your head off. Tone it down a bit. Last I recall I never invited you over here today. Don't come into my house and rudely yell at me about how bad of a hostess I'm being when you were never invited in the first place."

She ought to be having a bad day considering her tone. Admittedly, my tone matched her harsh one. I assume that she found her way to where I was by locating my voice. Taking a single look at me through the mirror she winced at the mere sight of me.

"You look like a train wreck. No, worse than that. You look like a dead person that has just dug her way out of her grave. What happened?" For a second, I thought that I caught amusement in her eyes. Disappointingly, I couldn't read too much into it due to the fact that the look quickly vanished.

"I don't know. I just kind of woke up like this." Although that was the truth, I said it as a question.

"Yes, everyone wakes up with a harsh bruise on their face and their skin stained red from what I'm guessing is blood that you had to wash off."

"Not everyone looks like a witch with long pitch black hair, chalk white skin, and a very bony structure."

"Wow, I expected a much better insult from you, Julia. I mean, I can tell you worked on that one really hard considering my name is Salem."

"Why are you holding a broomstick behind you? Hold on, let me see that. Oh, my mistake! It's just the stick up yours'." A slight smile edged onto my face.

"You should ditch your job as a psychologist and become a comedian. Since you're so good at making jokes." Salem rolled her eyes.

Her voice was laced with sarcasm. Normally, I wouldn't be short but with every word she speaks or I speak, it's like someone's driving a nail in my head.

"Salem, my head hurts so why don't you just tell me why you are here, and then please leave. I'm not in any state to entertain company."

"I told you. You said you had something to show me. You even made a point to make sure I understood it was important."

"I didn't tell you anything, not that I remember. Aren't you going to be late on your way back?" The sentence was aimed to push her out of my house. Unfortunately, Salem made no point to acknowledge my subtle suggestion.

"While I'm here you should tell me what's going on with that room full of children's toys and bedding. You don't even like children. Explain the whole dog situation too."

"My sister has a little boy. They will be coming over soon and staying for a little. Apparently, they will be visiting more frequently now. I had the space and money so I gave him his own personal room. As for the dog, the house was so empty. I'm human. I like company. Especially a dog's company."

"Okay Julia, whatever you wish. You know something? You should take down those crosses you have. It's not like you're religious. Besides, who needs that? If we are being honest, I think that is the most concerning right now. You have never been religious. Never. I'll help you take them down before I head back to that hell."

"Salem, leave them alone. This isn't your house. I don't see why you care." My tone was sharp and to the point.

"I just don't want you to be religious. You don't need that in your life. That whole thing is just, it's not good. Don't get your head stuck in the gutters." Salem had a pained expression on her face. For a second, I might have been fooled into thinking that she was sincerely concerned by my odd behavior. I knew she was only doing so as a way to grasp some control with me. When unfamiliarity arised with Salem she tried to change whatever that may be back to her own self absorbed version of comfort.

"Listen, Salem, leave what I believe in and what I have hanging around my house up to me will you? I don't need to be managed by you. I also don't think it's your place to dictate what I should and shouldn't do."

"Okay, message received. I will kindly back off, after this question. Are you feeling guilty about what you did all those years ago and are now trying to compensate. What is it, huh? Is it beginning to haunt you? Be real, Julia. It's not like what you did is going to warrant a demon coming down and dragging you to hell as a consequence. Those crosses, especially religion, is something you should leave alone."

"Get out Salem! Get out of my house and off my property now, or so help me God I will get you out myself." Anger shot through me as she struck a very painful and tender nerve.

Salem pursed her lips and angrily stomped out of the house. Her feet pounded against the floor with the weight of a thousand pounds. She slammed the door shut with great force. Consequently, the windows vibrated producing a buzzing sound. Anger bubbled my blood while hot tears blurred my already fuzzy vision. All of my emotions collided and crashed inside while I tried to keep my head above water. She knew it was a nerve to be left untouched. Instead, she hacked away at it like it was some game. The bloody audacity of her.

"Julia? What was that all about? What was she talking about?" Atlas's small voice filled in.

My fingers gripped the edge of the sink with such anger that my knuckles turned white and the edge cut into my skin. Staring back at me in the mirror was my own harsh reflection and Atlas's concerned one. Even though I heard Atlas ask me a question I knew that if I answered him immediately my tone would be angry, and he would experience misdirected anger, that he in no way, shape, or form deserved. Releasing a particularly slow and shaky sigh, I turned around to Atlas and rubbed my forehead. The sheer anger that I felt coursing through my veins made my headache worse than before. Grabbing tylenol, I took four.

"It's nothing that I care to explain or talk about. Do you know what happened to my head?" Unfortunately, my tone was flat, void of any life.

"No, I know that you woke me up while you were trying to get back into your bed last night. I tried asking you for something but I don't think you heard me. You weren't really acting like yourself so I thought that maybe you were too tired or something. Were you sleepwalking, Julia?"

"Not to my recollection. Then again, that's the point, you're asleep. Okay, I'm going to go and get some rest. Love, why don't you play with the dog or your toys?"

With a frown set in stone on my face, I slowly walked over to Atlas and lovingly kissed the top of his head. He frowned at me, most likely due to the lack of attention I was giving him today. Guilt set up camp inside of me while I looked at his down demeanor. Loneliness filled his precious grey eyes. The painful pounding insisted on occupying my head as I walked away to my bedroom. Closing my large door with gentleness, I crawled into my bed. Sleep soon took over my aganoized mind.

Twelve hours later, I rose from my slumber. The pounding in my head subsided in the tiniest measure. Holding my head, I ventured out from my room and down the dark stairwell. The only thing that prevented me from falling into the darkness of the night was the smooth polished railing. Each light step I took down (for I wished to let Atlas sleep) felt like a mistake. Isn't this the opposite of what ought to be done in the night during a house haunting? However, each time that thought sounded in my head my body protested and screamed at me. My limbs pleaded to be stretched. After landing my feet on the bottom step, I put the kettle on the stove. I popped a few more tylenol, and sat down on the couch to watch some television.

Eventually, my strained eyes strayed from the t.v. to the crosses on the wall. Questions filled my mind on what they truly stood for. Of course, it concerned God and Jesus. A symbol like that always stands for something much bigger with stories and a rich history. Why me? Why is this happening to me? All I am is a psychologist working in a psych hospital. I live with Atlas and don't talk to my family. My love life is as blank as a white sheet of paper. What was it about me that attracted this demon? If only I could end it all. Well, I can end it all. My phone rang obnoxiously on the seat next to me. The caller I.D. was unknown.

"Hello?"

No one answered. How lovely is this? Just what I needed. With an impatient tone, I decided to try one last time.

"Hello?"

"Julia…"

"This is she."

"I know that we haven't talked in a while but you're my daughter. I think you and I should have a visit. Don't you think? I'm getting old and I don't know how much time I have left. Although I don't approve of what you did it's in God's hands now. I think it's best that we just ignore it. You're not going to change your stance nor will I. Co-"

"Don't bring that incident up. I've heard enough about it today. You visiting isn't a good idea. Please don't call me again."

"Honey, I miss you so much, please. I just want to see you. Won't you at the very least think about it?"

"You know what, mom? Why not? I've been relieved off of work for some time now. It won't end until another couple of weeks. Given, If we can get along."

"Alright, I'll make my way over to you now. If I'm being honest I didn't expect you to answer so late at night. Why are you up?"

"Trouble sleeping, and you?"

"Oh, you know how it is. Old people are up half the night and then we go to sleep half way through the day. Get some rest will you? That way whenever I get there you won't be falling asleep on me."

"Alright, bye."

Since she is beginning to drive now she should make it mid day tomorrow. I sighed in reluctance to the future. She'll bring it up. It's in her nature. What am I to do with Atlas? I can't just ignore him for two weeks. Hypothetically, as long as all goes well. I'll have to put the bedding in the washer and make sure the room she stays in is nice and clean.

Easing my doubts about the future, I made my way to bed. A childish hope filled me, that maybe sleep would put all of my problems and thoughts neatly tucked away. Once I was halfway up the stairs I smelled something burning. Quickly running down to the kitchen, I located the source of the problem. There were paper towels next to the burner that had caught fire. Grabbing tongs to pick up the flaming ball, I threw it into the empty sink. Frantically, my hands turned the faucet on and let the cool water run over the towels, quenching the flames. Attempting to remedy my nerves, I went up the stairs and stopped to look in the bathroom mirror.

A burning sensation ran rampant in my side, nearing my hip bone.

Cautiously raising up my shirt, I saw the shape of an upside down cross that had been burned into me. Tracing my cold fingers over the unwelcomed symbol, I looked into the mirror with horror. Given how it was slightly healed, I assumed it to have been inflicted no more than a couple days ago. Cradling my head with my hands, I tried to remember why I woke up with a bruised and bloodied face. Different possibilities spun through my head, allowing fear to dance with it.

"Julia..." My name softly whispered out behind me. His voice caused my hair to prick at the back of my neck. Just as I had remembered, Wesly's voice was smooth as velvet, but that was only a trap. Fear rendered me useless. The very thought of him finding me caused my skin to crawl.

"Julia..." Once again the name was breathed out onto my neck, his hot breath violating my skin.

Chapter Seven

Golden Lights

HARSH FINGERS ABSENT FROM VIEW gripped my hands and another grabbed my shoulders with the force of a dead man. Black bruises of fingerprints imprinted on my forearm. Opening my mouth to scream, a thread and needle danced in front of my eyes. Heart pounding, skin sweating, eyes wide, and terror ran through my blood. Ducking under my bottom lip the needle and thread pierced, wiggling because it got stuck. The dull needle dug and thrashed through it as dark red blood spewed out. After a few moments of the needle mercilessly wiggling and thrashing, the thread tugged and pulled up against my raw flesh. Pain shot through me as it pierced my top lip with the same brutality and the process repeated while my lips finished sewing shut. My screams were muffled, condemning me to silence.

Once the needle sewed my lips shut, the hands that held my tortured body in place were released. Frantically touching my sore, blood ridden lips, I was horrified to meet my wide-eyed reflection Trying to figure out how to get the thread removed from my lips, I caught the few chunks of hair from my head ascending into the air in the mirror. Sobbing, I raised my hand up to grab the chunk, hoping that this would all end.

Breathing raggedly, I was helpless while my body slowly raised up from the ground. Tugging on the thick chunk of hair, I was released and collapsed to the floor. Blood dripped onto the tiled ground. A tall black figure loomed in the corner of the bathroom. Scrambling back up on my feet, I could once again feel chunks of my hair being pulled into the air. Without warning, my neck snapped back, following a painful cracking sound. What stood behind me yanked my hair so hard that it caused me to slam into the tile floor. Every bone in my body screamed with agony.

Forgetting about my sewn lips I tried to scream, only to violently tear at my flesh, causing more blood to flow through them. The sound gushed in my ears. Pain pulsed throughout my scalp. Looking to the side, I saw some of my hair falling to the floor like paper in the air. After a few seconds of soaking in the situation, another harsh tug at my hair was inflicted upon me. It quickly dragged me out of the bathroom. Instinctively, grabbing at the threshold, I prayed that everything would abruptly stop. My attempts were futile after it yanked all the more and dragged me down the stairs. Every step unforgivingly smacked against my ribs. Hot tears poured from my eyes, both from my pain and fear. Kicking at the ground, I violently clawed against the floor. My nails scraped against the wooden boards.

The invisible entity dragged me further and further to the basement door. The closer I got, the harder I dug my worn out nails into the floor. Pain seared into my finger as my nail on my pointer finger ripped off. Strings of flesh snapped, one by one. More tears gushed from my eyes like a broken dam. Just like that, it all stopped. Without any indication, it let go of my hair, resulting in my head dropping with a thump. Laying on the floor, puzzled, I recovered from my shock and ran to get up the stairs. Running into my room, I looked into the mirror on my wall.

Touching my swollen lips, I cried as I gently pulled at the string, foolishly hoping that it might come out so easily. Examining my bloodied, and tear swollen face through the mirror, I felt a desperate hopelessness. Repulsed by my own reflection, I stared at the black bruises on my arm, sewed lips, ripped off nail, and the bruises that laced my ribs as I held up my shirt. Hearing the sound of my door creaking, I turned around only to watch it slam close with a strength that shook the surrounding walls.

"Julia, are you okay? I heard the door slam close." Atlas's tired voice sounded behind my closed door. Hand over my lips, I remembered that I couldn't talk. Shakily walking towards the door, I opened it with a thousand emotions. One of them, ashamed that I had to inflict such an image into his innocent mind. "JULIA!" All tiredness was removed in his small voice and replaced with fear alongside shock.

"Julia! Come here, sit down. Don't move your head, okay? Just give me a second." Atlas's eyes were filled with an immense amount of worry as he carefully directed me to the couch in my room, slowly sitting me down. Raising his small hand, he traced them over my lips, grazing the thread, slightly tugging. Placing his hand down to his waist, he flashed me a reassuring smile. For whatever reason, the adorable dimples that showed on Atlas's confident face soothed my anxiety and pain.

"You'll be okay, I promise." Raising his arm up to my face once again, a soft golden light exuded from his palm and fingers. His eyes were fixed at the thread while the light grew larger and he ever so slightly brought his hand closer to my sewn lips. Closing my eyes, I allowed a fearful tear to escape my eye, tracing down my face. "Don't worry about it, I won't let you stay like this." Atlas's voice chimed in as he wiped my tear with his hand.

"Everything's fixed Julia." His words woke me up from the accidental slumber that succumbed me.

"What?" Surprised by the word that effortlessly flowed out from my mouth, I shot up to look in the mirror. The bruises, the missing fingernail, blood, and sewn lips were all gone.

"How did you do that, love?" Upon saying those words, I hugged Atlas tightly.

"Just some good spirit power, you know? I don't get to do it all the time. Since I'm just a kid it comes and goes. Well, not exactly, apparently, I have to have had enough rest for it to work. At first, I really didn't think I had to sleep but then I talked to the Big Man in my dream. He told me what's what. So now, I can protect you better. Isn't that really cool? I can shoot gold light from my hands like this! Pow pow!!!" Atlas shot the hues of light into the air, pumping his arms. Giggling at his cuteness, my eyes teared up from what must have been an extreme sense of gratitude and love. When I really thought about it, I loved Atlas like my own.

"What's wrong Julia? Did I make you sad?"

"No, no, no. That's not it. Atlas, you just made me extremely happy is all." Ruffling his hair, I walked him back to his room and tucked him in. Before leaving, I kissed his forehead and then went to bed myself. Taking three melatonin before getting under the covers, I quickly surrendered to sleep.

"Winston, get back here! You'll wake her up!"

Winston was the dog we had got. Jumping onto my bed, he licked my face and whined. Not all much minding his company, I pet him. Even if the dog's attention was warranted through his ability to sense my bad mood, nonetheless, it was welcomed. The dog nuzzled his head into the crook of my neck, blindly ignoring Atlas's calling. Scratching my head, I reluctantly sat up in bed.

"Julia, I'm so sorry! You see I tried playing ball with him but he just ran away and got into your room before I could get him. He is really fast."

"Don't worry about it, Atlas. We do have to talk though. My mother is coming into town. She'll be staying with us until my leave is over so long as all goes well between her and I. Don't worry, I won't be ignoring you at that time. You and I will continue our normal routine."

"Ohh, okay, if you don't talk to me then I do have the dog. When is she coming?"

"This evening."

"Can you and I go play fetch with the dog outside?" Atlas looked at me expectantly.

"Yeah, give me a second. I'll meet you outside."

He ran off downstairs but Winston stayed with me. He seemed like a couch potato. The dog sighed as I got out of bed, slightly pushing him off me.

"Winston, do you want to play fetch?" His ears perked up along with himself in much enthusiasm. "Okay! Go get Atlas then!"

While I was brushing my teeth and doing my hair I noticed a crack in the mirror. On the edges of the crack it looked like you could peel it back, almost like paper. My fingers hesitantly grabbed the edges that presented themselves to me.

With every little bit that I peeled back it appeared as though you could put your hand into a sort of abyss. Once I was finished peeling it all off, blackness laid before me. A strong urge to put my hand into it rushed through me. The blackness looked so comforting. I drew up my hand and put the tip of my fingers into it. Suddenly, I was in the passenger seat of my body, no longer calling the shots, hypnotized by whatever lulled me.

"One" Involuntarily shakily breathing out the word, I drew my hand up, only for it to be engulfed. Liquid covered my skin, yet none of it spilled out of the mirror. However, the ability to see my reflection continued in the darkness.

"Two" I leaned my face closer to it, daring to put some of my face in the mesmerizing blackness. Opening my eyes I could breathe in it. The cool yet soft liquid felt so inviting and peaceful. Everything in me wished to leave, but I was only presently a passenger, not the driver.

"Three" I climbed into the blackness. Not but 6 feet in front of me was a man sitting down. Walking towards him, I tapped on his shoulder. The man snapped his head back.

"Do you know what this is?" My voice was relaxed and sounded strange to me, as though it wasn't my own.

"It's all anyone ever needs. Julia, do you want to know something? If you just give in he'll give you everything you want. He gave me everything. I used to be so miserable. Now, I've never been happier." His voice was monotone and lazy. The inner me screamed as I sat down compliantly.

"I'm thinking of just giving up. However, I know I can't. My mother is coming back today. She will be happy to see me after the falling out we had. Every time I become so tired of fighting something like that always happens. Atlas came into my life and brightened it. Then it was the dog, and now my mother as you know. Enough about me. Who are you? You seem so familiar."

"Julia, I've missed you greatly ever since I left. I never stopped loving you. You were my everything and I left you. Do you know me now? I may look different but surely you know me by now."

"Wesly?"

"Yeah."

"Don't you dare tell me how you missed me, Wesly. Most importantly don't tell me how you loved me. What you did was never love. Tell me, please, do tell me how you beating me until I throw up blood is love? Was it your love that broke a beer bottle over my head, or whenever you broke my ribs? I want you to know that you're the worst person I have ever met in my entire life and if I just would have stayed away from you and picked up the red flags earlier my life would have been a thousand times better. I hate every bone in your body. Go to hell."

"Isn't that ironic? You're the one who is going to be dragged down to hell. I'm already here though. That's the difference between you and I. Is that you have to be dragged down in such misery. While I just went there willingly."

"Are you saying that we are in hell right now?"

"I am, you are not. He is just using me to get to you. It'll be interesting to see what will happen to you. You'll have to forgive me, Julia. I don't want to do what he forces me to do, nor have I wanted to say the things I said. The bathroom incident last night, he made me. That demon watched in the corner like we're some television show."

"One" His voice echoed.

"Two, forgive me Lea"

"What are you doing?" Panic filled me, the calmness was gone and my face filled with fear. Fear for the unknown.

"Three"

Pain filled my chest because of my quick beating heart. My head ached and my thoughts raced. Anxiety crept its way through my soul. Screams filled the space that I was in. Screams of tormented souls filled my head. Frantically covering my ears because the nauseating screams were so loud, I collapsed to my knees. They were pitched and filled with misery. Screams filled my head in such depth they consumed me. A warm liquid began to flow on the palms of my hands as a consequence.

I plead with God to stop the screams, but they weren't silenced regardless of how many times I begged. Desperate for comfort through the screams, I rocked back and forth. After they persisted minutes or hours, my sanity slipped like droplets of rain. Pushing through the agonizing pain in my throat, my screams joined the unseen others. My body couldn't decide on sobbing or screaming and soon they both mixed together. Misery drowned me and fear swallowed me.

I looked frantically for Wesly and for the first time in my life was begging that he would be there. Still covering my ears, I tried looking for him but he wasn't there. This went on for an hour, or I assume at the very least it was an hour. Time collided wherever I was.

Finally, the screaming ceased, and I laid down on the floor. I looked at my hands only to find very little blood on them. Cold threatening to take me, my body shivered violently. Goosebumps covered my skin and my teeth chattered from the frigidness. I need to think of something. Something good so I can cling to it in order to prevent me from losing myself. Thinking of Atlas and his dimpled smile, my eyelids began to feel like stone.

Chapter Eight
A Whole New World

ATLAS'S P.O.V.

AN OLD BMW SLOWLY ROLLED into the driveway. I squinted into the left window to see a poised wrinkled lady with short curly hair. Her face looked in question to me while she stepped out. At first, I suspected the old lady to have no eyebrows, but as she came closer, I saw that they were terribly thin. Maybe thinner than dental floss.

"Hey! Boy come over here." She waved her hand towards me. Why would she call me boy? Clearly, I'm the man of the house. The protector with sword in hand of the Great Julia Hellan Bettington! Subconsciously, my hands placed themselves on my hip while a cowboy stare took over my face. Then it hit me.

"You can see me?" I leaned in with eyes wide as Angel's halos. Biting my lip, I waited for her to answer.

"Of course, I see you, silly! Why don't you be a good lad for me and tell me if you know a lady named Julia Hellen Bettington. I'm looking for her. She's my daughter."

All defenses down, I jumped into the air and pumped my fists. A quiet

"Yes!" accidentally slipped from my mouth while I remembered I had to be cool. Straightening myself out as man of the house, I hid my excitement.

"Uhm I do know her. She lives here actually. Julia said she would play catch with me and the dog after she got ready. She hasn't come out for a couple of hours." Maybe Julia has grown tired of me and is hiding. Pushing my toes in the ground, I thought of how she might be better off without me. I need to try harder. I miss my mom. Not even my mom wanted me.

"Why the sad face?"

"You're mistaken. I'm not sad. I'll take you to her."

"You know, my hair used to be red like yours before I went grey. Curly too."

"That's lovely." Forcing a smile on my face, I shoved my hands into the pockets of my blue jeans.

Once I stepped foot into home, I felt a coldness that seemed off. Sometimes I wish that I was a bit older so God and the angels could upgrade my abilities. The glowing lights were said to be my early birthday present. Maybe if I was more useful to Julia, she would love me more. Even if she didn't, at the very least I would feel like less of a failure. As long as I could truly protect her, I wouldn't mind so much if she hated me. I swear on the crowns of heaven, Julia should be gifted someone better than me.

"Julia!" I called her name out with a curiosity that hopefully would grab her attention. Several tries later, and she still didn't answer. She always answered. "I don't know where she is. Last I saw her she was in her room.

Let me look around just a bit more. You can take a seat if you want. I'm sure she is nearby. She never did leave the house." I gestured to the couch.

"Why don't I come along with you? We can become acquainted while you search for her. I am ever so intrigued to learn as to how you and my daughter became so close. She doesn't like children. Last I checked she couldn't be bothered with pets. Julia always said she was too busy with work to care for them." With no time to argue against her, I nodded with my grey eyes in agreement.

"I know she doesn't like kids." Even though I asked Grandpa why, he never told me. He said I was too young to understand. I visit with him in my sleep. "Oh! My name's Atlas by the way. I didn't expect her to want me around or at the very least to talk to her. She surprised me with that. Julia has actually taken care of me really well. I don't mean the care as in clothes on your back and food with a nice warm house to be in. She goes beyond that. She comforts me and plays with me, entertains me, and makes me feel like I'm alive. Julia even goes as far as to tuck me in every night. She always tells me to be a kid and to not put myself in the line of fire. Although she hasn't actually said the words to me yet I think she loves me!" No, she couldn't love a nuisance like myself. Although, Grandpa said she did before I got my glowing lights.

At the thought of her saying I love you, I smiled so big that it hurt my face. Even where my dimples showed it hurt. I looked in every room and called her name. With each miss, I grew even more sad.

"Is this your room? Has my daughter given you a whole room to yourself. You even have decorations and all. Don't your parents wonder where you are?"

"Yes, this is my room ma'am. You see my mom abandoned me seven years ago and my dad never knew I even existed." Unfazed as I spoke, my sentences were rushed as I felt a cold reality set in.

"Well then, how foolish of your parents to give up someone so precious. At least you have a place now and someone who loves you. My daughter never really does say "I love you", but from what you have told me I'm positive she does. Julia tends to keep to herself so the fact she does all of that for you, a boy who used to be no more of a stranger to her, absolutely fascinates me."

"She viewed me as a stranger, but I never viewed her as one. Even if she doesn't love me I have always loved her." All of these people and spirits telling me she loves me started to make me doubt my disagreement. At the very least she likes me.

She hummed in response to me. Hoping to find her in one of the few rooms left, I gazed in shock at the bathroom next to Julia's room. Where the mirror used to be, there was a black liquid that showed itself as an abyss. The mirror was neither big nor small. It was just the right size for Julia to climb in with slight effort. I didn't have to see my face to know it was drained of all color. I could feel it. For the first time in my life, I felt like a hopeless and helpless nothing. I should go to hell. They need to place me in hell.

"What would that be, an illusion?" My throat started to close, and my eyes welled with tears. Some of them slipped and trickled down my cheeks. Big Man, just send me to hell. Even the whole of crowned spirits knows it.

The gatekeepers of Hell must be cheering for it. I don't have any right to cry. Biting my lip as hard as I could, I tried to shut the tears off.

"No ma'am. It's far worse. If only you would believe me."

"What's wrong?" She asked with a peaking curiosity.

"You wouldn't believe me even if I told you. There is no way! I should have been protecting her! That was my job. I was supposed to protect her and I failed. Now she is gone forever! Julia is gone. She won't ever come back and it's all my fault!" Wiping my tears, I scolded myself.

"Atlas, just tell me what's happening, okay? Even if you don't think I'll believe you, there is no harm in trying. Everything will be okay. You just need to take a deep breath, and take it slow."

Once my story ended, beginning on the night of her first nightmare too when things began physically happening and now, I waited for Chloe's response. She looked at me like I held the weight of the world on my shoulders. Her void of words made me nervously ramble.

"I've been here all along with Julia. I just never really let her notice me until the bad man came in and tried to hurt her. Can I tell you a secret that not even Julia knows? If I tell you then you actually have to keep it because I have to wait for the right timing. You can't even hint at her about it." Another tear slid down my face. Must have been the fear of rejection.

"Absolutely Atlas." Trying to reassure me, she patted my shoulder.

After whispering the secret into her ear, Chloe's eyes went glossy. Every emotion was painted on her face. That look made me nervous, so I fiddled with my fingers until she wrapped me in a tight hug. Had I been alive, she would have suffocated me.

"Now Atlas, I know that we haven't ever spent time with each other nor met but I'm so very happy that you are here and please don't ever leave. Could you tell me why you haven't told her yet?"

"She isn't ready for that. I think she'll need more time."

"Right, well as much as I would love to talk about this more, where is my daughter exactly and how do we get her?"

"She went into a world that the bad man created. The crosses weakened him along with the beatings, and his abilities were very limited. He needed a place where he could control the environment, where he could break her down mentally until she was weak enough for him to get her. He'll hurt her! It's already at least been two hours since. She's probably been in a lot of pain by now."

"How do we get her out?"

"I don't know. That's the thing, it's his little world. He can trap us in there just like he did her. There are way too many tricks of his that he can use on us. It's impossible to prepare for everything the bad man can do to us there. Ma'am, we can't do anything. I could try and come and get her, but I don't even know where to start, if I will be able to get out or how to do it. I know that I am a spirit, but I'm still a kid!" Worry overflowed me to the point my small fingers started to shake. A sea of emotions is what it was.

"Alright Atlas, I know you're scared, but if you and I can form a plan then I'll go and try to get my daughter back."

"No! He'll get you too! I think it would be better if I did it. No offense, but you're a human and old. Double the trouble." Running through the possibilities my breathing quickened.

"Knowing what I know now I can't let you do this all by yourself. My conscience wouldn't be clean." Anger at her naivete made me furrow my eyebrows. I, a spirit with powers, doubts my abilities to get her while this human with an expiration date, old, and vulnerable believes she can do it? Humans always overshoot their abilities. It's why so many of them die so young. Am I being too harsh?

"Okay, we'll have to make a plan then." Exhaling and dropping my shoulders, I removed the fear in my soul and replaced it with determination. Julia needs me. Chloe needs me.

JULIA'S P.O.V.

Waking up my wrist felt as though they had a weight on them. On the right wrist, a chain wrapped tightly that was grounded. Five feet of length was all it allowed me before the chain ran out of any slack. Anticipation for the near future pumped my heart full of adrenalin. Yanking the chain with all my strength, I begged it to break. Despite the rust that ate it away, nothing happened. Foot steps with a few seconds of leisure in between resounded in the blackness.

"Julia…"

His strangled voice spoke. Naturally assuming he was close, I tugged on the chain harder. For the first time in his presence, I wasn't scared. The adrenaline coursing through my thick veins replaced it with the courage to escape. Knowing that I was alone with no one to help me didn't allow for time to be scared. It was either him or me. Nothing was going to stop me from getting back to Atlas. Atlas has become mine, and I will hold him again. I will make breakfast for him again. I will kiss him goodnight again. Standing up, I wrapped some of the chain around my right wrist and held the slack with my left.

"I've come to get you. Those crosses were a dirty, dirty trick. You have made me very angry, Julia. If you wouldn't have done that there is a possibility that I would have spared you some of the torture. Despite the stereotype of demons, we will give mercy. You just had to have your way, didn't you?"

Gripping the chain harder, I put one foot in front of me and the other behind to add weight to my stance.

The demon's footsteps were loud and heavy as he made his way towards me. While his tall body came into view. I doubted my plan. Calming my stirring mind, I patiently waited until he came towards me. Three feet away and he lunged forward. My eyes processing the scene quickly, I stepped to the side after he was an inch away from me. Quickly looping the chain around his neck, I squatted and dug my heels into the ground, slowly going backwards so his weight wouldn't push me forward. His neck snapped backwards creating a crackle while his body did what I envisioned impossible. My heart thumped enthusiastically with glee at this. For the first time, I was in control.

His back snapped in half while I allowed my butt to hit the floor, simultaneously yanking hard at the chain. After his stomach hit the floor, me angled slightly behind him, the bone in his lower back protruding outwards. This time it was my turn to count on my own terms. Without skipping a beat I looped the chain several more times around.

"One." I placed my boot angled to the side on the top of his bone and quickly stomped down so it snapped again and touched the ground. A demonic growl passed his vile lips.

"Two" I stradled myself on his back and pulled with all my inner strength at the chain as I saw blood pour from his throat, the crown of his head coming dangerously close to his shoulder blades. Gurgling noises of him choking on his blood filled my head while the metal cut through his skin, accompanied by a gushing sound. The demon's head was now attached to his neck by a thread. Letting go of the chain, I walked to his hand and placed my foot on his wrist.

"Three." I grabbed his fingernails and quickly pulled them back so his wrist would snap. My heart leapt with joy. Revenge was a sweet treat.

Unwrapping his neck from the chain, I began to walk out in front of his limp body. Finding a weak spot in it, I hoped to break the rusted medal. The demon's hand grabbed my ankle while his body's bones snapped back in place. The blood from him retracting into the unholy vessel. Yanking my ankle, my chin smacked into the ground with blunt force. He began to pull me towards him. His head snapping back in its rightful position. Kicking with my leg, my toes smashed through his eye socket. A warm coating of blood seeped through my boot. A cracking noise later, I pulled my foot out to see brain matter carelessly attached. Getting up, I bolted in the opposite direction of him.

It wasn't three feet that I made it when the floor turned into water under me and I fell through. The chain snapped back at my wrist, keeping me strung in the air while the space above me turned back into a solid. There across from me appeared to be a hallway. In that hallway, flickering lights made it possible for me to see the demon at the end of it. He heaved heavily and smiled. The demon started to run in my direction.

With my other hand, I dislocated my thumb in pure hope that this would allow me enough space in the chain to let my hand escape. My body blind to the pain, I collided with the floor below me. Adrenalin soon shook my body. Searching the hallway, my eyes caught the demon edging closer. After quickly picking myself up, I fled towards the left hallway.

Once I came to the end there were three ways I could go. Forward, left, or right were my choices. Accepting the one with multiple rooms, I carved my way down the left hallway. Multiple rooms meant multiple havens. The rooms were labeled by numbers. A quick deliberation later, I chose number five.

Rushing, I opened the door and quietly shut it. I took a couple deep breaths and held my hand over my heart. I turned around to examine the room. A red colored light illuminated the space. It was empty except for a sink and mirror. Stumped, I wondered what the next step was. Clueless, I placed my head in my hands. Noticing a small outline of a door under the sink, I walked up to it and bent down to assess. There wasn't a way for me to move the sink or mirror, but whenever I pushed on the door it was so thin that it would go back a little.

Past viewing of horror movies told me to leave it alone. Crawling out from the sink a breaking sound erupted behind me. A hand clasped around my leg, and jerked my body towards the door. Feeling no claws, I questioned what would be with me. Shooting my hands to the legs of the sink, I went against the force. Realizing that the game of tug of war would end with my loss, I let go to grab onto the monster's head before shoving my fingers in its eyes. The release of his grip from pain allowed me my freedom.

Looked back to the hole below the sink. A black, slimy figure with bright red eyes and sharp teeth appeared. Only its eyes were stapled with holes from my infliction. While it was trying to crawl out, I broke the mirror with my hand, and grabbed a sharp long piece. Quick on his feet, the entity stood up. Smiling with his triangular tongue out, his head drew back as his mouth enlarged, an accurate imitation of a snake. He stretched his jaw as far down as it could go. The demon's eyes were absent from view. By the time he was done opening his mouth all the way, it took up the whole of his head.

With the glass in my hand I made a run for the door. Before I could even make it the demon threw me against the wall. I shrunk down and watched in shock as he stood over me. He grabbed me by the waist and bent down as though he was going to eat me. I took this moment to stab the glass into the roof of the demon's mouth. He shrieked in pain. Blood spewed out. Once he was far enough away from me, I seized the chance to run out of the door.

Turning to my right, I saw that the other hallway held the heaving demon with long claws. For a brief moment, I thought about giving up, just letting go. Where would that leave me? My mother would be heartbroken, and Atlas. The last thing I would want is to leave him alone. Somehow I ended up loving him like he was my own. Leaving him would be a terrible sin. Maybe it was best though. To leave, to give up. Coming back I would drag my mother into this mess. As for Atlas, he would be able to be a kid without having to worry and protect me.

CHAPTER NINE
HEAVY HEART

ATLAS'S P.O.V.

T HE SECOND CHLOE AND I formed a plan, we began to execute it. After I grabbed a bunch of the crosses and put them in a bag, Chloe and I crawled into the blackness. She seemed scared but she still put a brave face on. I think she did it for me. We held hands as we walked through.

"How are we supposed to find my daughter in this blackness?" Her tone held disbelief. You see, that's why you should have stayed.

"Well, I think there should be traces of her, you know? Maybe I could try and pick up on her and his energy and then follow that. It should work. Since we have all these crosses we should be fine. It'll act as a little protector thing." Giving her a smile, I continued to move forward. Don't worry, Julia. I'll find you. Eventually we came to a chain that stopped in the ground.

"I don't sense her anymore." I hate to say it, but it was the truth.

"Are you sure? She has to be around somewhere." Yes, I was sure.

"Once the chain stops at the ground, I don't sense her where we are. It's like she went somewhere else." I felt the tears begin to come, but I choked them back. Julia doesn't need me crying anymore than Chloe does.

"I could try something, but I wouldn't be able to take you with me. You would have to go back. I can't take you with me." Fear started to build in me.

"What are you thinking, Atlas? I can't just leave you."

"I can teleport to wherever her energy is. I can't sense it with us, but I know it's around here. I can't just take you with me or leave you here. If I leave you here, then he will come and get you. Please just go back, please." My eyes pleaded with her. Despite what I want, I don't have enough energy to teleport them both back with me since I stayed up all night last night guarding Julia's room. She would kill me if she knew I snuck out of bed.

"Alright, fine. If you don't come back soon then I'm going to have to do something." Chloe was very assertive when she said this.

I led Chloe back to the mirror and told her goodbye. She looked sad and hesitant. The moment when I got to where the chain was I teleported myself. There was a hallway in front of me and one on my right. Julia went to the one on the right. Eventually it led me to three hallways. She went to the one on the left, and then into room number five. I opened up the door and saw a hole under the sink. Maybe she went through there. Something doesn't feel right. If only I had more energy. After squinting my eyes, I saw a figure in it.

"Julia! Is that you?" I smiled and pushed back my feelings of something being wrong. I just wanted to get out of here with Julia.

"I can't believe I found you so quickly! I was so scared and thought you were gone forever, but you're here! We can get out of this place and play with the dog. Your mom is here, too. She was really scared for a second.

Did something happen to you? Your energy is different. Come out, Julia."
My voice sounded sad again.

Julia began to move a little which gave me hope. She started to crawl out. I backed up so she could easily move around. Her movements were slow and the more she came into light the more I realized it wasn't Julia. This was another demon. Thank God I have these crosses with me. He won't try to touch me now. I guess it's back to the search. Once I slipped out of the room, it became obvious that she continued down the hall.

Quickly, I followed the energy. I could sense that she was sad, scared, and tired. It felt like she was done and over with the situation. If she could just hold on a little longer then I could find her. I followed until I arrived at the end of the hall to a door. Hesitantly, I opened it. Julia's screaming rang through the hallway. Her scream was coming from the opposite direction. I swear on all golden brick roads, if Julia isn't okay, that demon will pay.

This made me incredibly angry. That demon knew I came in here and used false energy. I should have seen that coming! For all I know he did that everywhere, or the scream is just a distraction. Why did he have to pick her? Out of all the people he picked her. Julia is growing tired. I can feel it.

After a lot of debating I finally decided to turn back around and head towards the scream. The hallway went dark after a flicker of the lights. My vision failed me in this important moment. A growl erupted near me. I pulled one of the crosses out. Although I could not see, I still ran into the direction that she screamed from. Eventually, I smacked into a door.

Luckily, the impact left me unfazed. I took a second to make sure that this was truly her. Sensing the special bond, I smiled through my eyes.

My hand gripped the door knob tightly and I pushed it open. Julia laid limp on the tiled floor room that was lit by a green light. Tears poured down her face. Her skin blue as could be. Fear filled her eyes. Life appeared to be draining from her. A weak straining rumbled from her throat. The demon was hunched over. His hand wrapped around her neck. A white fog was escaping Julia's mouth, and being sucked into the demon's. Her soul. He was happily taking her soul.

Nothing could describe the amount of sadness I was feeling. My refusal to lose her again was the only thing that gave me strength to fight this. Quickly, I reached into my bag of crosses. In it, I had several cross necklaces that I could swing over his neck with some crucifixes. My secret weapon was a few that had nails going out of the back of them so they could be stabbed into something.

With one of my hands I swung a cross necklace around his neck. In the past, that would be enough to get him away but after taking some of Julia's soul and spirit he is much stronger. With the other hand, I stabbed one of the crosses into his flesh. A violent and intimidating roar erupted in the room. Even if he stopped for a second, I had to continue. Using the cross for leverage, I grabbed the front of the chain and pulled his head towards mine. Placing my hand on the side of his face, I mustered all of my strength to send him flying. He slammed into the wall. Sauntering over, I noticed his right side caved in. Pieces of his skull showed through. Digging my hand through the wound, he clawed at me but failed. Dragging him with my hand in his skull, I let go before his head hit the ground. He laid on his back while I grabbed the sides of face and slammed it into the ground, each harder than the next until it was half the size. Shouldering a lot of Julia's weight, I helped her out of the room.

Julia seemed to be going in and out of consciousness. My eyes teared up at the thought of losing her. What if he took too much from her? As much as I wanted to focus on that, I needed to get her far enough away. The crosses will only hold him for a couple of days. Until then, I have to figure a way out. Even being here will drain energy from Julia. She can't afford that. She will die if I don't get her out and soon.

I could feel the energy fleeting from her tired soul. Tiny traces of it continued to leave her as she gave up, slowly slipping away. All of my memories of Julia flashed back in my mind. They played in my mind like a quick movie. Reminding me of every smile and laugh we shared, each time we fought against the demon together, every time she tucked me in, gave me a kiss on the forehead, made me food, ruffled my hair, and even watched cartoons together. What I would give to play another boring game of uno with her.

"Julia, please don't leave me! I won't bother you as much if you stay. I promise! I'll do whatever you want. If you want me to go then I'll go, but please don't abandon me. Come on, Julia! Keep your eyes open! Please, I beg you don't leave. I need you. I love you. If you leave me all alone in this cold world, I will break without you." My voice broke, and now I could no longer be the strong little man that Julia needed me to be. I can't lose her again.

"Atlas, you'll be okay." Her breathing was short and her voice quiet. She spoke with strain. If she dies now, the demon will have her soul.

"No! You can't give up on me!" This was very true, she couldn't. Not again at least. Not here. Not now.

"Atlas, I love you." Life was draining from her. I could feel it.

"Don't say that! Dying people say that, and you are not dying! Julia, keep talking to me like you are now. I promise I can get you out of here. I can save you! I'm sorry I wasn't there any sooner. I failed you, but don't worry. This time I will not fail you." My sentences were rushed and my voice cracking. Tears flooded my sorrowful eyes.

It felt like ages before we reached the chain that was hanging from the ceiling. Even if I wanted to teleport her, I couldn't. This, of course, was a huge problem. One option that I could do would be to teleport myself up there and then lay the crosses on the spot above. Proceeding with my abilities, I could break the floor and pull her up. A loud screech sounded throughout the hallways. The demon from room number five was coming quickly.

"Julia, I'm going to have to leave you here for a second. Please don't think I'm going to abandon you. Just wait here and keep talking to me while I do it. Keep your eyes open." I could tell she was fighting.

If I rushed myself then it would be possible to get her up there. After teleporting myself up I laid the crosses down. The demon's footsteps and noises sounded closer with every passing second. My hands shook with fear of failing her again, of losing her.

"Atlas…" Julia breathed out. Her voice sounded scared so I assumed the demon was getting nearer, within eyesight.

"I'm trying, Julia! Wait one second! I need you to start standing while I'm doing this so I can use my strength to lift you up quickly!" I yelled out to her with urgence and care in my voice.

While trying to break the floor surrounding the chain, it was being very difficult. Maybe it was due to me being tired, scared, or even rushed, but regardless, it was almost impossible.

"Love, he's almost here." Her voice made it obvious that she was fighting to get those simple words out.

"I'm almost done." I kept a level tone so I could worry Julia less.

The floor around the chain broke and crumbled into the air. Julia was under the space obviously struggling to keep standing. I looked over as I reached out my hand for her to grab and saw the demon not but twelve feet away from her. He was running with great speed and screeched as well as growled in protest of not getting Julia yet. This was it, the moment of life or death. What if I couldn't pull her up? Hopefully, my spirit strength will allow me to do so.

Once she grabbed my hand I pulled her up quickly right when the demon reached for her leg. I sealed the hole and made it my next mission to find the mirror to exit from. During my search for the demon below, he pounded loudly on the sealed part with great force. It painfully echoed throughout, even on the floor we were at. Julia covered her ears with what remaining strength she had. Soon enough, I found the exit.

"Julia! I found it! We can get out now!" I turned around, and my smile dropped instantly. Julia laid limp on the black floor. Her eyes were closed and her breathing shallow.

"Julia?" My voice cracked as I ran over to her and began pulling her towards the exit. Her body was limp and heavy.

Tears dropped from my face as the reality of losing her sunk in. After pulling her through the black liquid of the mirror, Chloe saw her and grabbed her body to help pull Julia out. Chloe set Julia down on her bed. My heart ached as I hugged Julia's limp body with all my strength. Never in my life have I felt such sorrow and pain as I sobbed over Julia. Never have I failed so miserably for someone who I loved greatly. Listening in, the sound of her heart beat slowing more and more created profound sadness inside of me.

Chapter Ten

Heaven, Earth or Hell?

Atlas's P.O.V.

"ATLAS, I KNOW YOU ARE really sad and scared right now but calm down dear. Take a deep breath and calm yourself, okay? If you keep crying that hard you'll get sick."

"I don't get sick, Chloe. I'm a spirit. This is all my fault! If I had just noticed what was happening sooner she would be okay and smiling. How can I not cry? Besides, you're crying too." Rubbing my nose into my sleeve and wiping my tears, heartbreak was written all over my face.

"Dear, none of this is your fault. Are you the demon?"

"She's going to die. Her heartbeat is slowing down too much!"

"Let me call the ambulance." Chloe's tone was nothing but denial.

"Don't! The hospital can't help her. You need to leave now."

"I'm not leaving my dying daughter."

"You will." Using my abilities, I pushed her out the room without laying a finger on her and locked the door. This wasn't fair! Her heartbeat slowed to a full stop. "God, you have to help! Can't you see I don't have enough energy!? Why would you let me be here all this time for nothing! Help her! Help me!" My strong angry voice broke to a crack. "I just want her back."

Crying in the loud absence of her heart beat, a strong flick of golden light shot from my hands and eyes. For a second, it burned. Soft white glowing figures surrounded the bed. Twelve wrapped around towards me. Grandpa was at the very end. Except he had yellow light and wasn't a figure. He looked like he always did. Winking at me, he reached his hand out towards the right. The white figure to my right reached his hand out for me to grab. Grabbing hold, I started to turn into a golden-lit figure. The white, yellow, and golden lights grew brighter with every passing second. It grew so bright I couldn't see anything else and closed my eyes. As the room felt different, I opened my eyes to see everything back to normal. Me back in my body and Julia's heartbeat steady.

Grandpa looked at me for a second before leaning down to my height. "You know this won't happen again. Right?"

"Why not, Grandpa?"

"There's an order to things. You know that. It doesn't matter how important someone is."

"She's different."

"No, she isn't."

"Yes, she is. God wouldn't have helped if not."

"He helped because you're special." Grandpa lightly poked my chest. Looking over to Julia he spoke once more before leaving. "You're good enough to protect her. You are good enough. She's the one that must choose to stay." Unlocking the door, I let Chloe back in who was standing in front of it.

JULIA'S P.O.V.

A man sat in the room with me. Sitting in a large brown rocking chair that stood in the corner of the room, he shut his eyes, only to open them. My hands gripped the blankets out of expectancy for this to turn horribly at any given second. He rocked back and forth repeatedly, staring at me. His eyes were vacant of emotion and his face stoic. My mouth was dry and my body exhausted.

"Julia, are you alright? You seem so tired. Life was quite literally taken out of you. My condolences to you." Although his face held no emotion his voice was deep and filled with it, just like my late father.

"No, I'm not alright. Do you ever feel like just giving up?"

"Of course, but what is the fun of it all being easy? Life is hard, but when you fall you don't stay down like a coward. You get up, no matter how much it hurts. When you feel like you're crippled with terror you must be brave and push through it. Once you push through it enough times you will become above it. With each time it will be easier. If you don't feel like getting up after falling, then do it anyway because life doesn't stop for anyone. The longer you stay down, the longer life will beat you on the ground. It will hurt ten times more if you stay curled up in a ball. Get up, Julia."

"What did you mean earlier when you said "My condolences to you"? I haven't lost anyone."

"I'm glad you and your mother are getting along. Oh, how I miss her. Listen to me, Julia, you must prepare yourself when you lose her. When it happens please do understand that it is not your fault. My dearest daughter, you must cherish her before none of us can. Like I said, I have missed your mother a lot. She's a lovely woman."

"Dad, I don't want to lose her. That would all be too much. I can't do that." He sat up from the chair and walked over to my bed.

"Julia, you are so much stronger than you think. My dear, you may not know it, but you have gained something that will carry you through it. What you have gained is priceless and yet you are blind to it. No matter though. Soon enough you will gain the knowledge of knowing what you lost only to recover. After that happens that one thing will outweigh everything else immensely. Wait, a little longer."

Kissing my forehead, he gave me a warm smile. He disappeared right after that. When I thought about my mother leaving, a great sadness filled my soul. A bitter smile came to me because although I was sad I couldn't imagine my soul large enough for the pain after the demon's take. What is it that is waiting for me? There is Atlas, mother, Salem, Winston, and my house. Atlas is so sweet and adorable, my mother I loved dearly, Salem was someone who I have known for years, and that dog is a bright joy. Like always, my father couldn't be further from the truth.

"Julia, if you wake up then I can tell you a secret of mine. Not now but soon. I think you'll be ready soon. You just wait a little."

Atlas's voice rang through my head as I started to wake up. Seeing my father could have been a dream. If it is, mom should be perfectly well. Trying to open my eyes seemed next to impossible. They felt like a heavy weight, refusing to lift. Through great determination, I was able to lift the veil of stone that was my eyelids.

"Atlas, you don't need to try and bribe me to wake up, love." My voice was groggy and my throat terribly dry.

"Julia! I can't believe you're awake! I missed you so much! You have no idea! So did the dog, but I missed you a whole lot more. If I'm being hones,t I thought you were going to leave me." His voice was filled with cheer as he hugged me tightly

"Leave you? No, I love you too much. How long have I been sleeping?"

"About a week, it was for a long time. Most of the nights I slept here to make sure nothing bad happened to you. While you were under, I fixed that thumb of yours."

"A week?!" At most, I expected two days.

"Yes, calm down a bit or you might pass out. It will take awhile to get your strength and spirit back. Don't worry though, I'll give you lots of my energy." Worry filled his face.

"Thank you for getting me out, love." Gratitude held my tone.

"How could I not? It was my super strength that did it though."

"No, you did it, Atlas." I ruffled his hair.

Atlas started to run out of the room and yell for my mother. Suspense began to rise within me while I thought of what to say to her. Where do I even begin? Hello mother, I'm so glad to see you after seven years of absence. Let's go and get a drink. No, that's not right. Wait, stop. Did Atlas truly call for my mother? Has he made his presence known to her due to the situation? Taken by surprise, I remembered how adamant Atlas was with his rules. My head spun thinking about all the talks and memories I had to catch up on.

"Julia? Are you alright?" My mother's voice echoed off the walls. What would possibly be an appropriate response to that? No, getting my soul sucked out of me was really enjoyable, or Yes, I'm perfectly well and fine despite all things considered.

"Yes?" My answer sounded like a question rather than a statement.

"So, I know about everything that's been happening. Atlas caught me up on it all. Don't be alarmed though, I believe every word of it. The child didn't show himself to me. For whatever reason, I was able to see him. You desperately need to take it easy or your health will decline greatly. Don't be foolish and do something beyond your capabilities given the situation. You have Atlas and me to help you until your strength is restored. Keep your activity to a minimum. I don't wish to lose you."

"Oh, may I go downstairs?" Internally cringing at my own response, I began to sit up. Once my feet hit the floor, I was reminded of their lack of use in the past week. Consequently, I caught myself on the bed and tried to gradually put my legs back to work.

"I don't see why you couldn't. Julia, please don't be so formal with me. I've missed you greatly. You're my only daughter, and if you are ready, I would like to put the past behind us." Peering into her ice blue eyes, I felt reassurance.

"I would like that as well."

Giving me a warm smile, she urged me to come downstairs as she had dinner ready. Even though I didn't feel back to normal, I did feel better. Once I got to the dining room, I sat down at the table. It was odd how I didn't see my mother for years yet, the atmosphere was like when I was a child. Coming down from a long rest and smelling the breakfast that she made me. Waiting at the table while rubbing my eyes in a hopeful attempt to rub the sleep away. This was better though.

What I had now was so much better. Atlas and his dimples, my dogs begging for food at the edge of the table, my mother's smile, my beautiful Victorian house, a stable job, and a feeling of overwhelming contentedness as the aroma of joy and peace danced throughout the air. Out of all my twenty eight years on this earth, never once have I felt as though the stars aligned in exception for me. Yes, things were hectic, and crazy, and mind blowingly odd, but underneath it all I could not deny that what I had before me was something that I refuse to lose, something that all my love had been given too. My love for what surrounded me in this very moment as Atlas dug in his pancakes and my mother laughed at the dog with such joy couldn't ever be matched with anything else. All of my love is here.

"Julia!" Atlas said with a big smile. "These pancakes are so good! Have you tried them yet?" His eyes glanced down to my untouched food.

"No, I was just about to put some peanut butter on them. You should try it, it's really good. Here, have a bite of mine." He looked at the food with such doubt and question, squinting his eyes. As if he thought the food was poisoned he took a bite with such caution. Once Atlas started chewing them he smiled widely and grabbed the peanut butter to put on his pancakes. Before I was even halfway done with my plate, Atlas finished his and went out to play with the dog. My mother looked at me with tender eyes and a knowing face.

"Mom, I'm sorry. You have no idea how sorry I am. When you told me not to do it, I should have listened to you and now look at the mess."

"Julia my dear, nothing you could do would ever make me stop loving you. While you may feel guilty, I have already forgiven you and so has Someone else. All there is left to do is for you to forgive yourself and move on. Don't let it consume you." She grabbed my hands and held them tightly. I didn't expect that reaction.

"Alright, let me get the dishes." She smiled at me and said she would help.

Continuing with the dishes, I watched as the dogs chased Atlas around and although I couldn't hear him laughing he very obviously was. Once Atlas couldn't out run Winston, he began teleporting from place to place. The dog eventually gave up on the chase and laid down in the grass. In response to the tired action, Atlas laid down with him. The small boy's head rested gently on Winston's stomach. He picked up a dandelion off the ground and blew it as the white pieces drifted into the air.

"Why don't you go out with him and I'll finish up the dishes for you. It looks like you want to spend time with the boy."

"Thank you, mom."

She nodded her head in response and took the plate from my hand.

With caution, I walked up to Atlas and the dog so as to not disturb them. At first, I thought Atlas was asleep because his eyes were closed but when I stepped on a leaf that crunched under my footstep he opened them and smiled.

"Do you mind if I lie down with both of you, Atlas?"

"No, you can help me to pick out shapes and animals from the clouds. Here, I'll scoot over. Be careful when you step over that rock. It wouldn't be good for your health if you fall."

With effort, I was able to nestle my way next to Atlas. It didn't take long before he began to spot animals and things from the clouds. Each time he found one he became quite excited but tried to whisper as to not wake up Winston.

"That one looks like Spongebob! Do you see it, Julia?"

"You have a really good eye for this stuff. Yes, I do. Oh! Look. That one looks like a whale. Don't you think?"

"Mhm."

After some more time of spotting different forms and shapes in the clouds Atlas had fallen asleep. His breathing was peaceful as the sun began to go down. For a second, I just laid there. Maybe it was because I felt deeply blessed to have Atlas in my life or due to the wonderful scenery that laid in front of me, making no effort to conceal it's beauty. The sky was now filled with hues of orange, red, and yellow. Flowers bloomed across the whole lawn and not too far off were the trees of the forest and their leaves a deep green. Due to the light breeze, the blades of grass bent at the tips just as the leaves of the tall trees rustled quietly, offering their own sounds of peace.

Once I breathed in the fresh air that calmly filled my lungs, I quietly stood up and swept Atlas into the comfort of my arms so as to not wake him. Carefully, I carried him to his room, being mindful to miss all of the creaky floor boards. In fear of waking him up, I tiptoed out of the room and with great caution closed his door.

Chapter Eleven
Damsel in Darkness

TELEVISION SOUNDED NICE AT THE moment. I decided to go down and watch some. My mother stayed for ten minutes before she too went upstairs to fall asleep. After another hour, I decided to head off to bed as well.

"Julia, I had a bad dream. Can I sleep on your couch?" Atlas's voice ripped me from my relaxing sleep. Without opening my eyes I could tell that he was standing outside of my door waiting for me to answer him.

"Atlas, would it help if you took Winston to your room?" Even if I knew what was going on in the house. I could tell by Atlas's voice, it wasn't the demon, rather a bad dream. At some point in time, he did have to learn to sleep in his bed after one. That's what my parents did with me.

"No." His voice changed from a sleepy tone to a cry within a matter of seconds. Such a fear that arose within his voice in that single no caused my heart to break for him.

"Okay, come in." Despite a groggy voice, my worry for him was tied in with it.

A creaky sound etched in the cold air as the old wooden door slowly opened. The click of it closing soon followed afterwards. Little footsteps running across the creaky floorboards kept in rhythm before Atlas's weight slowly sunk into the mattress, causing me to dip down with him.

"You said you were going to sleep on the couch, not in bed with me."

"I'm sorry. It was just really scary."

Atlas began crying to the point his whole body shook the bed. My heart broke for him as he trembled. Turning my body towards him, I hugged him tightly in hopes it could protect him from all the danger. I kissed his forehead and rubbed his back while telling him everything was going to be okay. His sobbing ceased, but he still held onto me for dear life.

"Julia?" His voice broke the silence.

"Hmm?" My response was tired. No matter how much I wished to stay focused on the boy, I couldn't. Getting half of my soul taken away from me, quite literally made it next to impossible to keep my eyes open for a long period of time. Especially when waking up from a deep sleep.

"You have something on your cheek." Atlas's voice was leveled and clam.

"Oh, what is it?"

"I don't really know, but let me get it off of you."

Atlas's fingers went up to my cheek. He held them there for a second. Slowly, I was falling back to sleep under the warm covers. Oddly enough, his fingers traced my cheek for a long second. Only a moment away from falling back asleep, Atlas's nails seemed to be growing thick and sharp.

"Atlas?" My shaky voice concluded that doubts filled my mind. Opening up my eyes, I saw the demon laying next to me. His toothless smile filled my vision as he let out an evil/amused laugh. The skin on his head bubbled and bursted with puss. His acid inflicted skin rubbed harshly against mine as his long, pointy white nails cut against my face. My heart threatened to burst out from my chest at the rate it pumped, wishing to escape itself.

My screams filled the air as his thick nails were being pressed violently into my eye sockets, pressing further and further down. Gushing along with popping sounds violated my ears. I thrashed around and gripped the burnt hands that rested on my face as long nails were pushing my eyes into the very back of my head. Blood gushed down my face as my throat filled with pain from my loud screams.

"One" The demon's voice filled my head.

"Two" He began laughing loudly the more I thrashed and screamed in sheer pain.

My body thrusted forward as I woke up drenched in sweat. I gasped for air as my hands went to my eyes and checked to see if they were absent. After frantically feeling for blood on my face, I came to the conclusion that I was physically okay. Despite me telling myself that I was okay, my heart and breathing didn't agree and continued with their rapid pace. Quickly scanning the room with my eyes, I found that I was luckily alone.

"Just a bad dream, a bad dream." I repeated to myself like a broken record in a futile attempt to calm myself down.

After breathing out a long sigh of anxiety, I laid down again despite my heart violently pounding. With every little noise or creak, I shot up in my bed again. Eventually I was too terrified to close my eyes in the dark so I turned my lamp on. Within the time span of thirty minutes, I heard creaks in my room again. My eyes slowly opened as I balled up the dark blue sheet in my hands to such a degree that my knuckles turned ghostly white.

"Three" A strangled voice spoke.

The black demon was on the right of my bed, and the burnt one on my left. No matter how hard I tried to breathe it seemed impossible. Once I recovered from the initial shock, I desperately tried to run out of my room to where all the crosses were. The burnt demon with bleeding eyes grabbed the back of my shirt and pulled me to the bed. Each grabbed one of my arms and held me down. A long knife was in the hand of the black demon. He drew his arm up and began to plunge the knife down. Before it even penetrated my skin, I screamed with all my might. It's sharp point stabbed painfully into my skin as I felt it tear at my insides. A gasp of pain and a tear escaped me while I felt the knife go all the way through, piercing my spine and going into the mattress. Tortured screams filled and scratched at my throat, releasing themselves all at once. Each demon cruelly laughed as they both took hold of the knife and slowly slid it up. The knife cut through my skin, spine, and organs like they were nothing until it reached my breasts. The blood from my body escaped and pooled around me as I drowned in it. My own gurgling noises filled those sad ears of mine.

"Julia! You're okay! Wake up!"

I woke up to Atlas shaking me and my mother looking at me with sad eyes. Immediately upon waking up, I sat up and burrowed my head into my knees while I hugged my legs and heavily cried.

"Atlas, why don't you head out of the room, okay?" My mother asked him with a soft voice.

"But…"

"Come on dear, it'll be okay. Just give us a moment alone."

"Okay, fine." Atlas's voice sounded sad and reluctant.

Refusing to look up or move I continued to cry into my knees and hug myself. My mother tried to comfort me by telling me everything was going to be okay and wrapping her arms around me. At this moment, I wasn't solely crying out of fear. I was exhausted. This was cruel and confusing. It was exhausting to have a nightmare and then waking up but not truly and then to have another nightmare but actually wake up the second time around.

The whole situation made it confusing. It produced raw terror and self doubt. At some point in time, my mom was able to calm me down and I was close to normal again. Atlas knocked at the door and asked if it was okay to come in.

"Go ahead, love." My voice sounded tired and quiet.

As he walked in the room, my mother mentioned something about going to get me a cloth and a glass of water. Atlas looked at me with sorrow as he walked over to my bed.

"Are you okay?" His innocent face was filled with burden.

"I'll be okay soon. I'm sorry that you had to see me like that."

"Don't be sorry. Was it the bad man again?"

"Yeah." My voice broke and Atlas crawled into the bed next to me, giving me a hug.

"I know this probably doesn't help you but he can only mess with you in your dreams for now. The demon is too weak to do anything else."

"That does help, Atlas. Thank you for coming to wake me."

"You're welcome. Are you sure you'll be okay?"

"Yes, I think that if I take melatonin and sleep in the living room then all should be well."

What happens after this thin veil of protection is torn from our little world? What happens when the demon's strength is restored and every atom in his body is burning with an intense hatred along with rage that is magnified by a thousand? Do I just live every second in extreme and utter terror? Terror that bites at my worn skin until it eats it's way in, poisoning my blood before rising to my heart and freezing it cold… shattering. Following in suit, I'll be six feet under. Shoving each overflowing thought painfully down where it escaped, tucked away in a locked chest bound by chains, I suffocated the thoughts. Despite the irresponsibility of it all, it kept my mind sound. Worrying is a long treacherous road that leads to a dead end, entrapping you within a whirlwind of uselessness. Soon enough, genuine plans will pump my slowed heart, leading that mind of mine.

Fresh thoughts tauntingly danced in my mind, eager to be entertained. Walking downstairs, running my soft hand against the rough and cracked bubbled white paint on the wall, I accepted the thoughts about work dancing in my mind. Doubt joined with as I thought about how I was to properly help my patients, packing their massive envasions of life, right along mine. An overflowing mind will press spitefully against the skull until it explodes. Finding comfort in the light thump of my steps, I remembered once again that a trainee was to come. Mary assigned Salem or I to supervise and teach. However, neither of us were in the same work as him. Another perk of a psych hospital run down to the ground without a single care, training those that don't belong in your work.

Reaching the couch, I let myself fall into it. High off stress or relaxation, time slowed as gravity pulled me down to the seats. Closing my eyelids as I studied the crosses on the wall, my body found the cushions of the couch, allowing itself to be enveloped by it. Soft strands of hair fell onto my face while the comfortable blackness of sleep made me its passenger.

Beams of sun fought their way through my closed eyes and woke me up with urgency, accompanied by the ringing of my phone. Taking but three seconds of squinting before I could comprehend the words spelled out on the screen, I groaned with reluctance. Work dared to stir my quiet mind that usually refused to do so. Was I supposed to go in today? With annoyance I accepted the call.

"Hello?" Barely succeeding, I pushed the grogginess in my voice down and laced it with a professional one.

"Julia, would you mind coming in today? I know that I said tomorrow but you see, we really need you here. The other psychologist that was filling in for you left. She said she was finished working here."

"Why?"

"She wouldn't really tell me why."

"Are you sure, Mary? You don't have a clue as to why she abruptly quit?" Lovely Mary was undoubtedly holding back a highly pivotal piece of information.

"No..." Her tone left room for nothing but argument.

"I'll be late, but sure."

After hanging up the phone and tossing it on the couch, I started getting ready for work. Maybe, I should quit too. Surely, there is something better awaiting than this. I'm astonished the psych hospital hasn't been shut down yet, considering all of the incidents that have happened. Whatever did happen to my fill in, I'm sure that it was another one of those. Mary probably didn't tell me due to the fact that she needs someone to be there.

"What are you doing Julia?" My mother asked me as if I was ten.

"I'm going to work." The more I talked the more I realized my tone was sharp.

"You shouldn't be back until tomorrow."

"You're right I shouldn't, but not everything that should happen does happen. It's not a big deal. It's only a one day difference." I rubbed my hand against my forehead and let out a sigh so I could soften my tone.

"You seem upset about it even then."

"Mom, I love you, and I'm sorry that I won't be able to be with you for the majority of the day. You came all this way just for me to work. I could be back by five, seven, or even nine. Please watch over Atlas for me."

She seemed slightly disappointed by the situation. My keys clanked and turned in the ignition as I began my way to work. Easing myself into the seat, I thought about how at the very least this would leave me no way out of resolving things with Salem. Once I arrived at the psych hospital, Mary was there to apologetically greet me. Disappointingly, Salem wasn't to be found in my line of vision. Agonizingly, I moved on to my next patient.

"Hello Ezekial, how are you today?" Somehow, the poor man lost more weight. How could that be possible? All of his skin clung fearfully to his bones the last I saw him. Now, his skin looked paper thin... two seconds away from his bones snapping through. An inch all around his eyes was rimmed with a harsh crimson red, more than usual. Three clumps of hair bravely didn't waver on his scalp. Every little movement he made was unforgivingly accompanied with a pop sound of the fluid breaking up around his white protruding bones.

"Dr. Bettington, he made you bleed didn't he? I told you so. That evil black blood of yours poured from your damned soul! Oh how I hold seeing you tortured to my dear soul. For all you know, mine is gone. You seem tired and exhausted. I'm exhausted too! They won't leave me alone! The help that I need is nothing that you can give me. Did you bring him here? No, I won't slit that prettty throat of hers! Shh, oh, tell me then."

"Are you talking to me or something else?" He tugged and pulled at what little hair he had left.

"Something else." His voice was filled with anger right alongside fear. Ezekial's bloodshot eyes darted to the corner of the room and back to me.

"Do you want to tell me about it?" For the first time since I met him, he looked hopeful.

"He's tall and mean. It has long nails and burnt skin. He'll take you like he took me. My life is nothing now. He's almost finished with me, I can feel it in my bones Doc. Can you save me?"

"Ezekial, whenever this comes back and tries to take you over I want you to try something new for me. If it's possible, think of all the happy thoughts that you have ever had happen to you in your life. Fill your head with those memories the best you can. Let's try it now." No matter how much I wished to help him, I couldn't. Even if I knew what he was experiencing was all real.

"Something happy? I remember when I was seven or eight my father used to make the greatest macaroni and cheese and so I would beg him to make it for me, and so he would. It didn't matter if it was a good or bad day. As long as I was able to come home to my father as a little kid and he made me my favorite food, then it was all okay. It's just little things like that."

"That sounds very nice. Would you mind telling me more?"

"Dr. Bettington, to answer your earlier question, I think I'm doing better."

"I think you are as well. Why do you think you're doing better?"

"I'm accepting the reality." This produced a smile out of me. Not the fake ones that I give my patients in order to help them but rather a genuine one.

"Ezekial, once you start accepting what's real and what isn't, then we can begin your journey to a life outside of this hospital if you continue to truly get better. Don't give up, okay? You're so close. Even if it's hard, you have to keep pushing for the better. Ezekial, you're strong and capable. If you keep going like this then I can assure you that things will start looking well."

Soon, Ezekial left my office. After talking to more patients, I realized that it was time for my break. The breakroom was empty but I went ahead and ate my food. Salem walked in no later than five minutes, she looked like she had a lot on her mind.

"Since I was overstepping whenever I went to your house, I won't make you get me another ramen." Salem's version of an apology was never a true one, but that was her sincere version.

"Seems fair enough. Do you know when the new guy is coming?"

"Julia, he is already here." She looked at me with surprise.

"Since when?" My head snapped up and my eyebrows furrowed. No, I was sure he didn't come in until, oh never mind.

"Since last week. I've been training him. I doubt he is going to last. Truly, his spirit is so upbeat and happy all the time. With that type of personality he'll break in such an environment."

"Maybe he will or maybe he won't. Regardless, it'll be someone new. Did you at least warn him how low grade this place is?"

"No, he'll figure it out soon enough. Even I figured it out, so did you and everyone else who works or has worked here."

"Don't you feel bad about not saying anything? The least we can do is give him a head start on running away from here."

"You could always leave, Julia." Salem looked at me with piercing eyes but covered it with a soft tone. She knew I wanted to leave and always pushed me to do so. However, alike everyone on this planet, I have bills to pay and mouths to feed, not to mention my attachment to my patients who rely on me.

"No, I'm making great progress with Ezekial. You can't just up and leave multiple patients who have come so far with you. Especially ones like these. These people take so long to gain trust with, let alone a relationship. If I left, the vast majority of them would regress."

"Alright, whatever floats your very considerate boat." She flashed me a kind smile.

Salem clicked her heels out of the room and off to her own job. Before I finished my meal, I realized that I needed to give papers to Mary. Not just a few papers, a few box loads of them. Quite frankly, they were long overdue. Walking softly against the tiled floor, humming to a light song, I made my way to Mary's office. My grip repeatedly slipped on the brown cardboard handles in the hallways. My tired fingers continuously found themselves ever so slipping from the poorly made handles. Trying my best not to fall flat on my face, I peered around the boxes that stacked over my eyes and hesitantly walked. Upon rounding a corner, I bumped into someone and the boxes escaped my grip which caused all of them to fall over and papers flew in the air, patiently making their way to the floor. My eyes stayed glued to the papers that scattered the hallway as I spoke.

While kneeling down, I said sorry in one sigh that sounded more exhausted than I intended too. Some of the papers fell from their folders which meant I would have to go back and organize them all over. It's not like I could do such a thing in the middle of the hallway. Now I had to haul the boxes back to my office. If only I had paid more attention then I could have gone home by now. I'll have to stay longer. Instead of a sigh, I yawned.

Chapter Twelve

Hide and Seek

"Here, I'll help you." A man's voice that was unfamiliar to me had spoken with joy residing in his tone. This provoked me to look up. His hair was black, although it wasn't very long I could tell it was curly. His eyes were a stormy blue compared to my green.

"Thanks, you must be the new guy." Trying my best to produce a courteous smile, I suppressed the groan of homesickness that threatened to escape.

"So I am. Sorry about that just now. I got a little distracted." Manners for a worker here is fairly taboo, especially given it wasn't his fault.

"Don't worry about it. After I sort them out again, it'll be fine." Letting out a chuckle, I got started on repairing the damage.

Picking up all of the papers, he and I threw them into the boxes. After the mess was cleaned, we both stood up. This is my chance I thought. Salem should have mentioned something to him at the very least. He interrupted my thoughts by reaching out his hand and introducing himself.

"It's nice to meet you. My name is Roman."

"Pleasure to meet you, Roman. My name is Julia. While I have you, I need to correct a mistake my friend Salem made. She didn't warn you, but if I were you I would stay far away from here."

"What do you mean?" A suppressed smile broke on his face.

"The psych hospital is so understaffed that everyone has to work overtime all the time and sometimes they still need more hours from you. None of the supplies here are actually updated to where they should be. Unfortunately, many patients escape and hurt the workers due to the poor supervision and lack of training. For instance, while I was off, a psychologist that was filling in for me abruptly quit. Mary won't even tell me why. So I assume she is trying to cover up what happened like she does with all the other instances. The only reason I'm here is because I care about the patients and their health. You're not emotionally invested into this job yet, so escape before you have something holding you back."

"Hmm, I'll think about that." Amusement had gone from his expression. Rather, doubt wavered in his blue eyes and then was concealed with a roaring confidence.

With a nod and smile, I picked up the boxes. Feeling like my arms were about to give out, I took a second. Attempting to juggle and shift the weight of the boxes to carry them, they threatened toppling again. Roman swiftly lifted them up into his arms.

"Oh, thank you." Giving him a smile of appreciation, I rubbed my arms as we walked. Being home with Atlas and mother right now would be great. A nice movie, popcorn, and a soft blanket would truly do wonders.

"So, what do you do here?" Roman's voice strayed me from my thoughts.

"I'm a psychologist. My goal is to help the patients get grounded in reality enough where not only they can leave this miserable place but also function in society to the best of their ability. As for the ones who will never be able to get out, well, I'm just there as a support system that helps them deal with their diagnosis."

"How many patients have you rehabilitated?" Curiosity peaked his voice.

"Since I've been here? Ten, I've helped ten people get back to relatively normal lives." Such a low number made me feel like a failure.

"Huh, So you have to stay here and organize all of them again?" Staring at him in a brief second of confusion, I realized he was talking of the papers.

"Yeah" My sigh soon followed my reply.

"If you wouldn't mind me staying to help I would like to. This is my fault anyway."

"That would be amazing." Briefly, I thought about fighting him on the grounds that it wasn't his fault, but I desperately wished to go home.

Roman and I reached my office and began organizing them. We mostly small talked and chatted about what drew us to the careers we chose. Roman began to ask me something but cut himself off and paused several seconds.

"What is it?" Putting the papers down, I looked at him expectantly.

"You said Salem was your friend, correct?" Hesitation held his tone.

"Yeah…"

"Please don't be offended by this question. Doesn't she seem off to you? Even in the slightest?"

"If I'm being completely honest, the Salem other people know is different from the one I know. Salem and I have been friends since the seventh grade. During highschool years she changed like everyone else does. She grew up a little more and became slightly more mature, but also reserved. At that point in time, she was a good person. People change after they get their degrees and experience life on their own along with careers, but she never did change. It's impossible for a person not to change throughout the years whether it is for the better or worse. Since I haven't witnessed it, I know she acts like the same old Salem around me. Beyond that, I don't really know what type of person she has morphed into. From what some people tell me, she is far from the Salem I know."

"You guys haven't drifted apart since then?" Now it was disbelief that held him.

"No, we have. Although we may not be as close we are still relatively close. Did she do something to you? You said she was a bit off." Going back to organizing the papers, I kept my ears open for his response.

"She just gives off a bad vibe. Something seems wrong. Have you ever met the type?" Paying attention to the organization of my papers, I waited for Roman to follow in suit.

"Yes" A click of the light switch snapped in the air causing the lights to go out. All that presented itself before me was an uncomfortable darkness that held secrets. A threat to our lives matched it. The air around turned to a harsh heat. Was this a preview of hell?

"Roman?" Calling out his name, I began to feel an uneasiness rise and bubble in the depths of my stomach.

"Yeah?" His tone was ever so placid. Looking over to the direction I knew him to be, my eyes could make out his tall silhouette.

"On your side of the desk there should be a drawer. More specifically the third one down. In it is a flash light. Could you please grab it?"

"Sure" Saying the words with such ease, I hoped the events I feared were about to unfold would put themselves at ease as well.

The sound of his hands rummaging around in the drawer in an attempt to find it filled the silence. Pens and pencils smacked and clicked against the wall of the drawer. Papers crumpled as they were smushed together. A few small bags of chips shuffled. Just when I heard his fingernails scrape against the bottom of the drawer, the click of a flashlight sounded. Following in place, a beam of light offered what little light it could to give hope in the darkness. Roman's low and flat humm eerily clashed with the silent space between us. The tune hinted with familiarity. Yet no answers popped in my mind. For once, my overworked mind froze. My blood ran cold at the sound.

"Can you please stop humming?" The fearful crack in my voice joined the hairs that stood up in unison on the back of my neck.

"I'm not humming. I thought that was you." Only then did it click in my mind that the tune being hummed was of the hymns that played in my car and again on the television.

Trying to slow the erratic breaths that escaped me, I shuffled closer to Roman. Being with humans in a time like this usually made it feel all the less scary, even if only a microscopic amount. Roman looked into the dark with confusion as the humming continued violating the once peaceful air.

He scanned the room with the flash light to no avail. That hopeful beam of light that gave a false sense of comfort flickered. On it went for three seconds, off for one second, on for two, off for one, on for one, and then dark once again, staying dark. Sounds of Roman hitting the flashlight against the palm of his hands sliced through the air. Heavy footsteps hit the tile floor from the hallway, sounding with anger as they approached my closed door. Praying that my eyes would adjust at a quicker speed, I stared in fear of the same door opening. Hearing my heart pound violently in my ears, I tried to calm myself. That poor heart of mine wished to leap from my chest and escape the danger.

"Roman, turn the flashlight on." My voice was slightly shaky giving away the fear I was trying to keep under control. I made no attempt to keep my eyes averted from the door.

"It went out." His voice was leveled. If he had been through what I had, he might just be in sheer terror with me.

"Try to turn it on again." He pushed the button again but with no use.

Tauntingly, the door slowly creaked open. Every little movement the door made was an opportunity for it to creak louder, taunting me slowly. Despite it opening, no footsteps followed it.

"Find another flashlight." This time I sounded rushed and impatient.

Roman didn't answer, but I could hear him rushing to find a flashlight. The door ever so slowly creaked open even more and a tall figure loomed hunched over in the doorway. My breathing was now rigid and my whole body froze. As though the figure aimed to taunt me, it stood there for several seconds in the darkness.

"Julia, do you see that?" Now, the man sounded scared.

"The thing in the doorway?"

"Yes."

I hummed in response as that was the only thing that I could produce in my frozen state. Atlas said he was still stuck in that world. The demon disappeared from the doorway and footsteps pounded as the door slammed shut creating a boom that echoed in the room. At this point I could hear Roman's breathing quicken. Once the door slammed shut with brute force the footsteps stopped soon after. I frantically searched the room with my eyes, but failed to catch a glimpse of anything.

"Roman? We need to leave." A knowing tone filled my voice.

"What is going on?" If I wasn't mistaken his voice was fearful but it was obvious he was trying to keep his fear in check.

"I can't explain to you but we just need to hurry up and leave. Give me your hand."

Roman grabbed my hand as soon as he spotted it in the threatening darkness. He and I frantically ran to the doorway before the flashlight on the desk lit up. We stopped momentarily to look at the thing that caught us by surprise. Our eyes hesitantly followed the light which lit up the wall near the door. Black liquid imprints of feet were revealed in the illuminating light. From the shadows that it caused, I could barely see Roman's face. He looked appalled more than anything. My guess was that he couldn't and didn't want to comprehend what was happening. A sound of someone crawling resounded as our eyes followed the black foot prints against the wall onto the ceiling. Once my eyes laid upon the figure who was crawling on the ceiling, all of those rightful fears of mine came to life as they were encouraged by the justification. Puss from his acid burnt skin dripped from him to the floor, burning holes to the ground. Those long white nails scraped and tore at the ceiling.

The demon started racing towards us against the ceiling. No matter how much I wanted to scream, it was futile. My hand jerked at Roman's the moment I tried to make a run for the door. To my surprise, we made it out of the room, but the hallway offered us no light either. Our footsteps hitting the floor were loud but those of the demon's crawling in a run towards us was quicker.

After we rounded a corner I could no longer hear the demon behind us and took the chance to go into the breakroom. Swiftly opening the door and closing it, I held my hand over my heart as though such an action would calm the raging storm inside. We crouched down into a corner away from the door. The only noise in the room was us breathing heavily. After a few seconds, we were able to get it under control in fear that if we continued to be loud the demon would inevitably hear us.

"What is that?" Roman's whisper was more of a very quiet yell.

"Shh, what if he hears you?!" I also whisper yelled as a subconscious response.

"That thing, no. That is not a he. It's not human." Roman was right in a way. However, that didn't matter. What did matter was the fact that both of us were two minutes away from death.

"Roman, please I beg of you to be quiet." I turned my face towards him so he could see how desperate I was. Whether it was pity at the sound of my voice cracking and the desperate look on my face or he didn't want to get found himself, he went quiet. I realized that we were tightly gripping each other's hand. I released my hand from his.

Humming filled the halls once again which made what little sense of security I had go away. The lights dramatically flickered in the hall. All that went through my head is that I was going to die along with this poor man who I had accidentally dragged into the midst of it all. If anyone should die it would be me. Roman was just being a good person and helping out. The footsteps became nearer with each second. The door to the break room opened and the demon walked in.

"Julia… I'm back."

His strangled voice spoke with such glee in the torment he was causing. He knows where we are. He's just toying with me. Coming to this realization, my hopes plummeted. I looked at Roman who was wide eyed and filled with terror. An idea popped into my head. The majority of me doubted it would ever work, but I couldn't just sit idly by.

I looked at Roman and grabbed his hand again. Hopefully, he would trust me enough to follow. My eyes glanced over to the door and then to Roman before I started to cautiously crawl towards it. When we got to the counter of the breakroom, we were halfway to the door.

"JULIA! DO YOU HONESTLY THINK YOUR GAMES WILL WORK ON ME!?" His voice was filled with rage and boomed loudly.

Each and every one of the tables and chairs in the breakroom flew across to the side we were on. A few had clipped our shoulders. The lights flickered on, giving a halo of confidence. As quietly as we could he and I tried to crawl out the door to the left. Using my hand, I motioned for him to go first. He shook his head while I mouthed "please" to him with a desperate look on my face. After an agonizing few seconds went by, he reluctantly went first. I knew that the demon was going to get me, but it wasn't right to drag Roman along with.

My body soared like a rag doll against the wall. While my helpless body was flung through the air, the door slammed shut with a lock. Like clockwork, once I smacked into the wall the light bulb brightened by a 100 shades until the glass burst into the air. A shattering sound went off twice, once when the glass broke around the bulb, and another when the small pieces of glass hit the floor breaking into a thousand small pieces. The demon started to crawl on all fours towards me. My body shook with grave fear. Roman pounded on the door from outside. I could hear his body slamming harshly against it to break the barrier down. With each slam of Roman's body, the demon grew more agitated. His face grew hard and cold. All in less than a second, he turned to the door with a loud growl. Without touching it, he made the door fly off it's hinges and quickly walked towards Roman, grabbing him by the collar. My knees gave out from under me as I tried to stand up in a pathetic move to help him. The light to the hallway flipped on which aided in what little I could see.

CHAPTER THIRTEEN

ANSWERED PRAYER

⊰⊱⊰◆⊱⊰⊱

"**J**ULIA? YOU'RE ALRIGHT, AREN'T YOU?" Atlas's face was in front of me while calmly talking.

"Yes, I'm okay." My heart warmed at his dimpled smile. Pulling Atlas a little closer, I gave him a kiss on his forehead.

"Let me go take care of this, okay?" Atlas patted a bag that was on his side and walked away.

His small body walked over to the demon and pulled a cross caked with sharp ends of nails sticking out in several places. He stabbed it into the demon's side torso, and gripped the weapon fiercely before taking it out only to plunge the sharp cross again. Blood splattered across the white painted wall. Atlas snapped the leg from a chair and swung it hard against the demon's ankles. Falling backwards to the ground, Atlas grabbed the glass coffee pot and broke it against his stomach. The glass pieces crunched, pricking their way inside his skin. Crouching, the brave boy lowley whispered something into the evil spirit's ear. Rounding up his fist, he punched the roaring demon across the face so hard that black bile sprayed from his mouth. He picked the demon up by his arm, threw him over his shoulder and let the demon harshly slam onto a table, breaking it in pieces. The demon groaned while Atlas picked more nailed crosses from his bag. Shock filled me as I watched him grab two nailed crosses and stab both of them into the demon's eyes. A painful screech erupted from the demon. Atlas took this chance to reach for a crucifix and shove it down the monster's throat.

Choking on it, the evil creature swiped for Atlas's small body but failed to hit him. Atlas's face filled with a rage that went million miles deep as he pinned the demon down with his small hands. A golden glow began to emanate from his right hand. At the streak of it, the demon's skin burned off the bone. Atlas put the golden illuminating light onto the demon's chest, pushing down farther and farther creating a deep burned hole. Sizzling noises filled the air. He traced his golden lit fingers across the evil's body until skin and flesh seared off, leaving strictly bone on the demon's arms and face. Black blood and clumps of skin were left on the floor from the assault after the screeching demon independently left.

"Someone tell me what was that, and what just happened? Who is the little boy with a bag of crosses?" Roman looked astonished and over the situation.

Where do I begin? How do you summarize something like this? Well Roman, I'm sorry to inform you, but it appears that I have dragged you into my little demon-trying-to-steal-my-soul dynamic. Hmm, that actually might be a good way to do it.

"Are you a religious man, Roman?" He stared at me for a second before answering.

"Yes, I mean how can you not be after seeing something like that?" His hands motioned all around him.

"What you have witnessed was a demon who is trying to take my soul, and this is Atlas. He is what you would call a good spirit. Essentially, he is here to help me, but he has become a part of the family." That sounded about right. Normally, I wouldn't dare to tell another living soul about this but the poor man was just traumatized.

"Atlas, did you show yourself to him? Did you break a rule? Could you get into trouble for breaking one? You're okay right, love?" Those were only a fragment of the questions that filled my mind.

"I didn't show myself to him. There is a second way people can see me. It's a special rule. I can't tell you though. I'm okay. I promise. You should see if Roman's okay though. He looks shocked."

"Why does a demon want to take your soul?" That was a valid question to ask.

"If only I knew Roman. Then I wouldn't have a demon after me." I chuckled at the end to cover up the stress and worry that filled me.

Roman looked perplexed. After I explained a little more and went into detail about everything, he seemed to process it better. He asked many questions while Atlas cleaned up the place. Like me, I'm sure he won't fully come to terms with it until he experiences more. Hopefully, he doesn't.

"Julia, can we go home soon?" Atlas looked at me with a tired face. Ruffling his hair, I told him that I would be out soon. Since I felt bad about abruptly leaving him in such a shock, I gave him my number, so that we could continue the conversation later.

Atlas and I got into the car and drove home. While I was tucking him in for bed, a question popped into my head.

"How is it that only certain people can see you, and others cannot?"

"If you're talking about Roman and Chloe then I'm not sure I can tell you. If I do, it might reveal everything." Atlas winked with a giggle.

"You're keeping secrets are you?" I smiled at him in amusement. If there were things he couldn't tell me, I was fine with it. Everyone has their secrets.

"Maybe, maybe not." He said it with a playful smirk. All of a sudden his face turned serious.

"Julia, do you love me?" For a brief moment his face was filled with worry.

"I love you to the moon and back." If anything it was an understatement.

"But, you don't like kids." His voice was heavy with burden.

"Oh, you're right. I do not like kids but you are a very special child. For a very special boy like you, I'm more than willing to make an exception. Listen love, you are very special to me. In the span of time that you have been here, you've become my whole world. You're very right when you say that I don't like kids, but for whatever reason you're different. You are special to me, and I can't begin to express how grateful I am to have you in my life. Don't doubt it for a second."

Once I gave Atlas a kiss on his forehead I went to call my mother. Going back down the stairs, I made sure to keep my footsteps light so Atlas could fall asleep faster, trying to miss the creaky steps on the way. Finally arriving at my red kitchen and picking up the phone, I wondered why she hadn't been here since we arrived home. The telephone made it's comforting dialing tone as I tapped my foot in anticipation for my mother to pick up. After what seemed like an eternity she answered me.

"Yes dear?" All of my worries drifted away as I noted the calm tone in her voice.

"Where did you go, Mom?"

"I decided to visit some old friends of mine in town. You were out so late that I thought it would be good to use the time to visit with them instead of waiting around. When did you get home?"

"Oh, about ten or so minutes ago. I just put the kid to bed. Well then, I won't keep you. Have fun, Mom."

She hung up the phone after saying her goodbyes. Looking at my clock, I realized that it was eleven. "The Office" was on as I poured myself a glass of wine. It was well deserved after the day I had. With great enthusiasm, I grabbed the fluffy red blanket from the closet and curled up under it on the couch. This was bliss, I thought. My house was perfectly warm but the blanket added to it and the wine went smoothly down as the show played at a volume not too loud or too quiet. The lights were dim and I was extraordinarily comfortable.

When I was ever so close from falling asleep a loud knock started on my front door that made me jump from under the covers. Reluctantly, I rose from my half dazed state and away from the comfort of my couch. Before I opened the door, I yelled out to whoever was there, asking who it was. Salem's voice answered back to me. I swung the door open.

"Salem? What are you doing here this late? It's 12a.m.!"

Upon looking down at her face I cut myself off once my eyes met her puffy and red skin. A tear escaped from her eyes as she stood on the outside of my doorstep. Immediately, I gently grabbed her arm and pulled her in. Salem never cried. Since this was the truth if she were to cry it was something extremely serious that needed to be cared for at once. Salem often kept her problems to herself. On the rare occasion that she even hinted something was wrong, if you didn't seize the moment to see what was happening, she would just smile and act as though nothing was wrong. Timing with her was everything.

"What's going on?" I looked at her with concern as I threw a blanket over her shoulders and guided her to the couch.

"Julia, what am I going to do?" She put her head into her hands and cried harder than she was before. I went to fill a glass of water for her, but soon joined her on the couch.

"I'm sure whatever it is, you'll be able to get through it. Did someone do something to you?" She lifted her tear stained face from her hands and looked at me with hope.

"You've gone through it. You would know. Julia, I can't have this baby. Please walk me through your abortion so I can be ready when the time comes." My face went pale as memories of the incident came flooding back.

"Baby?" The word was said with such astonishment and fear under my breath. Salem shook her head.

"Salem, don't do it unless you are sure. Ever since that day, my life changed and not in a good way. Every day is filled with such guilt and sadness. There is nothing more that I wish to do than turn back time and change what I did. I changed my mind right before I laid down on the table. Even though I knew I switched my decision, I couldn't move. Every bone in my body felt so heavy despite my heart and mind screaming for me to leave. Then they put me under and it was too late." Grabbing her hands, she ripped them away from me the second I touched them.

"Julia, just because you had a miserable experience doesn't mean I will! You have lived in misery but I will not! The least you could do as my friend is encourage me in this hardship. Instead you're just relaying YOUR miserable life and guilt on me. You changed your mind. I'm sure of my decision. This is my body, my choice."

Once she said this, I stood up from my couch.

"You asked me to tell you my experience and I did. It was miserable. You can't get pissed at me for telling you my honest opinion when you asked for it. My life is not miserable, rather the choice I made and the repercussions that came with it. I'm trying to help you. Whether or not you listen and take into account what you witnessed from the aftermath of my experience is up to you. What I had and have to go through, I would never wish that upon anyone else." Salem got up from the couch, as well.

"You are being so selfish right now! Unlike you, I'm not an indecisive bitch who's a coward. Unlike you, I know what I want. Your experience is nowhere near mine. I'm not some sick freak who was getting an abortion to spite someone. Fuck you, Julia, and fuck your pretentious act." She heaved in anger.

My eyes pricked with tears after all the memories and pain of what I did came to the surface. I marched towards the door and opened it.

"I just wanted to make sure you were sure of your decision so you didn't regret it. Get out." She appeared stunned and stood there for a moment.

"Are you serious?" Salem looked more pissed than ever.

"Get out. Now!" All of my emotion boiled inside and resurfaced.

With a huff of annoyance, Salem left and I shut the door. My feet felt like cement as I walked up the stairs. With every few steps, I paused due to the crushing feeling that was rising up in the pit of my stomach. After some time, I reached my room and pushed open the door so lightly that it did almost nothing. Slowly, with tears streaming down my face I slumped down one of my walls. All the thoughts raced through my head. Each sentence I spoke was accompanied with a pause and sob.

"My poor baby! I could have taken care of my child. My baby is all alone and gone because of me! I ended you so late! I threw you away. Oh God! I want my baby back. Please, God, please, just give me my child back. Let my baby be okay. God! Let me be with my child. That's all I want! I just want to hold my baby. I need to see my child's face, just please God. I'll do whatever you want, if you just let me hold my baby. Let me hear my child coo and giggle. Let me cradle and love my poor baby. Let me watch my beautiful baby grow."

The words struggled to come out as I sobbed into my knees. Repeatedly,

I begged for my baby. My body shook with regretful sobs as my feelings overwhelmed me. Everything I repressed was fighting to get out all at once. The tears poured down from my face. My body shook with such violence with every tear that escaped. Now it became impossible to keep my thoughts at bay. I killed my perfect baby. My baby is dead.

Barely, I could hear my door opening. My mind could not get off of my child. No matter how much I tried to stop crying and collect myself it was futile. All of my emotions and thoughts smothered any strength or ability to get a hold of myself. I silently hoped it was the demon. My death would give me ease. Why did I freeze? I knew I wanted to keep my baby and I failed to get up, let alone utter to stop.

"Julia? Don't cry. Listen, I heard you crying about what happened. You don't have to be sorry anymore. I love you, okay? I've forgiven you. At first, I didn't tell you who I was because I was scared you would tell me to leave if you weren't ready. I'm sorry that Salem told you before I could. Please don't cry, I never want to make you sad, at least not like I did before." My head snapped up to Atlas's voice. Tears continued to stream. My heart broke more, if that was even possible.

"Atlas, what do you mean? Tell me what you mean please." Atlas looked down with sadness. Hope clung inside me.

"Well, I mean I don't want to make you sad like I did before I became a spirit. I'm sorry, I did it again. You're crying like you used to."

"You're... you, you're my..." At that moment I stammered as the reality sunk in. Atlas nodded his head. My poor baby.

Quickly, my hand wrapped around Atlas's as I pulled him into me and hugged him with all my love. I hugged him tightly as I cried and kissed him on the cheek.

"Atlas, I'm so sorry. My poor baby." Shock caused my tone to be leveled and quiet. Finally, with a rush, my emotions broke loose. "Please forgive me. I love you so much. I'm sorry, Atlas. Don't be sad because of me. It isn't your fault that I'm crying. Please don't think that." Atlas's arms were wrapped around me tightly just as mine were to him.

"Then why are you crying?" His voice was muffled into my shoulder.

"I was crying because I hurt you in a way you never deserved. Knowing I wanted you, I did nothing. You were and are my baby and I treated you like you were nothing. Every single day since has been filled with regret because I wanted you more than I have ever wanted anything, yet I was too scared to do anything. The things I said about you, what I did to you, was the greatest sin I have and will ever commit to you and myself."

Atlas lifted his head and looked at my tear stained face. What if he remembered the horrible words that poured from my mouth as though they were meaningless? All of that hurt that was surely inflicted on him if he does. Those words must have felt like acid burning into his skin. His poor soul.

"What are you thinking?" Atlas's small voice broke the silence.

"Did you hear what I said about you, or at least remember what I said about you while you were still in the womb?"

"Since I became a spirit, yes. If I would have been born then I wouldn't have remembered." His face was filled with sadness.

"Atlas, I meant none of it, please I beg of you to not think those words were anything more than anger, misdirected anger."

"Who were they meant for?"

"Your father, but instead I took it out on you."

"Did you love me?"

"Yes."

"Are you sure?"

"At the time yes, I said horrible things, and did worse but regardless all of my anger and hurt smothered the love for you and because it was easier for me to look away from the truth, than it was to face it I kept looking away from reality. The reality that I loved you, wanted you, and that you were not your father but my perfect child. Every atom within me was fighting for you but my mind was fighting ten times as hard for reasons that were easier to accept and to see what I wanted, but not what I needed. By the time I made my mind up that I wanted you, it was too late. I could have done so much more."

"What was my father like?"

"He wasn't kind. Your father loved to hurt people. No matter the relation he had with them, he hurt them as bad as he could. I left him before I found out I was pregnant."

"Did he hurt you?" Atlas looked at me expectantly.

"Yes, a lot."

Atlas appeared as though he was finished with the questions. I can't believe I have my baby. This was my baby. How does he still love me? How did he forgive me? Why isn't he angry with me?

"Love, why do you still love me after everything?"

"Because you're my mom." He said the words with a broken heart.

That one word made me feel like I was being pushed off a cliff. A single word put me into momentary shock, blowing me away. I was left to absorb the fact that not only did my child still love me, but also that he considered me to be his mother. No, I heard him wrong. I don't feel worthy of such a title.

"Atlas, you're perfect. You're absolutely perfect. You are so kind, loving, forgiving, generous, adorable, smart, funny and just utterly perfect. You know that even before you told me you were my child I loved you just the same and you became my whole world quickly after I met you, or for the second time at least."

"I love you too!" Atlas hugged me tightly and showed off his dimples.

"Do you want to go watch a movie?" Hope hung on a cliff in my eyes that he might want to spend time with me.

Once he shook his head yes, we went down to the couch to watch our movie. Atlas fell asleep curled under the warm blanket not even thirty minutes into the movie. With extreme caution in order to not wake him up, I scooped him into my arms and carried him into his room. After planting a kiss on his forehead, I tucked him in and went back to my room to fall asleep.

Chapter Fourteen

Secret Enemy

Seven years ago

Anger filled every inch of my body fighting to explode and spill out. My vision was only red and my feet were heavy as I walked up to her door. The rain poured down with all its might and refused to let up. My rage spilled out as I swung it open. Consequently, the door knob slammed violently on the wall. She had no right. We glared at one another. Nothing would be left unsaid after today. I slammed her front door shut. She opened her mouth, ready to explode, but I stopped her before any syllable could escape from her.

"You have no right to tell me what to do. You have no idea what I'm going through."

"Do you realize how selfish you're being, Julia? What did this baby do to you? It isn't that idiot of a guy you chose to stay with because you were too scared."

"Scared? Chose to stay? Are you serious right now? Why in hell would I have chosen to stay with him? I was stuck and terrified and weak from how much he hit me every day. Do you have any idea how many times I was left bleeding out on the floor, clinging to life? Don't ever tell me I chose to get abused. I got out as soon as I could and when he could never hurt me again. I was smart about it."

"You know what, Julia? You're right. You didn't choose to stay there or deserve to be hit. You should have had the abortion in your earlier stages! I told you to get it done as soon as you found out! That baby has a heartbeat, little fingers, toes, and brain activity now. It is an innocent baby who does not deserve to be murdered because it's inconvenient for you, or it's hard, or even that it's not what you wanted. Julia, you're a mother."

"I hate this baby just as much I do to it's father. I could care less what happens to it. For all I care, it could burn in hell along with it's father. Nothing about this piece of shit entices me. So what? It has a heartbeat, toes and fingers etc…. I hate it with every cell in my body and will do everything in my power to see it be ended. This thing is by far the most worthless, waste of life, idiotic, disgusting, and piece of trash that I have ever encountered. There is no way that I will let it live. It is an extension of Wesly. I don't care what I have to do or how. I won't allow it."

"Oh, Julia, you couldn't possibly mean that. You couldn't possibly be that…"

"That what? Tell me mother."

"That evil."

"Really, evil? If that's what you believe then fine. I'm evil. Okay? Is that what you want me to be?"

"Never, Julia I know you. No matter what you're going through you wouldn't say something like that about a human being and truly mean it.

You're already twenty six weeks along. Please, I beg you. Go to therapy and work out your problems with a therapist and I'm sure your opinion of this would change about your child."

"His child, not mine."

"Julia, this baby does not carry the mistakes of it's fathers. The baby is your beautiful child who will never turn out like him. Don't punish a child for its father's mistakes. You can tell yourself all you want that this child is his and will turn out like him to make yourself feel better about your choice. You can't do this."

Without a word, I walked away as the tears began falling down my face. I made no effort to shut the door as the rain pounded outside.

-Present time-

My body woke up in a cold sweat. For a second I didn't place the heavy breathing in my room as my own. Worry for Atlas motivated me to get out of bed and check on him. Lightly, my feet hit the floor making no sounds as I made my way to his room. With the slightest push, I opened his door a little more to be able to get a better look at him. He appeared as though he was sleeping in heaven. His face looked so peaceful while he was snuggled into his covers. My beautiful child. Warmth filled my soul as all of the memories with Atlas played in my mind. A smile spread across my face as I looked in awe at this child with me, my beautiful baby boy.

Reluctantly moving away from his door, I went downstairs. A few of the steps creaked in protest under my weight. Taking in a breath of gratitude, I spotted the dog in the living room. After petting Winston, I put the kettle on the stove, waiting patiently for it to finish boiling.

"Julia." The whisper cut through the air clearly.

Without hesitation I turned around and looked for the source of the voice. My eyes scanned the room and the stairway carefully trying to catch any abnormality but failed to find anything. Although my heart skipped a beat, and it felt like I was betraying my own safety, I turned around back to the kettle. I'm near the crosses. I should be safe. My phone rang impatiently, causing me to jump.

"Hello?" My voice sounded sleepy and slightly fearful. Nothing was answering in response. The only thing I could hear was the dull hiss of static.

"Hello?" Still dead. I decided to hang up the phone.

I only wanted some tea. Why is that too much to ask? A nervous sigh escaped me. Winston woke up and began walking towards me. His adorableness calmed my nerves. Before I could pet him, he walked away. The water rumbled in the kettle, begging to be turned off. My hand moved to pour it in the green mug but the dog's growl stopped me. Slowly, I turned my head to his direction.

"What's wrong?"

He eagerly stood at the front door. Hope flared in me that he might only need to go to the bathroom. For a second, I thought I might have to battle the demon tonight once again. Winston ran out the second I opened the door. The cold air from outside bit at my skin. Once I shut the door and poured my pot of tea, I went to let the dog back in.

"Winston!" My voice yelled with strain hoping that he would come back.

His absence was deafening. The moment I found a flashlight my search for the dog continued. After trying to find him in the front and back yard, but failing, I assumed he ran off after an animal in the woods. Atlas would be devastated if the dog was missing. I stood deliberating, but finally I decided to go look for him in the forest.

The leaves crunched loudly under my feet. Twigs snapping under my weight as I walked through the forest calling his name. I hugged myself tighter while the cold wind consumed me. Leaves from the trees rustled as they shook, barely revealing the full moon that loomed over the forest. Darkness covered every tree and blade of grass as I walked along. Unless I had the flashlight, my ability to see wouldn't have been made possible. Every few minutes my body responded to the cold in the form of a violent shiver.

"Come here, boy! We need to get back inside where it's warm and cozy! I'll give you a treat or two! Okay, five treats but that's only if you come here by the time I count to ten. One, two, three, four, five, six, seven, eight, nine, te-"

I stopped counting the second I heard him coming my way. He can look forward to five treats which seems excessive, but it is what I promised. My speech must have sounded enticing enough. After all, how can a dog turn down so many treats?

"Come here!" The walking stopped.

"Winston?" A thump and then a whine erupted from behind the bushes that laid in front of me.

Without thinking twice about it I ran to where I suspected him to be. He was laying on the ground with his eyes closed. I gently shook the sleeping dog while saying his name. All of the things that could be wrong with him ran through my head. My arms wrapped around his cold coat as I lifted him.

"You'll be okay. I'll get you some help soon." My voice was slightly high to aid comfort in his sweet heart.

The hairs on the back of my neck spiked up. Something felt wrong. I looked around but didn't see anything so I figured I was being paranoid. A twig abruptly snapped from behind me. I gently let the dog down and attempted to look at the source.

A rope was tossed around my neck and jerked back tightly. Without a second of delay my throat squeezed closed. My breathing became strained as my heels dug into the ground while my feet kicked violently. My hands grasped at the rope trying to claw it away from my neck in order to give it some slack. Gasping for air, I used my hands to feel around for whatever was behind me. It only took a few seconds to realize that what I was touching was not a demon.

My hands reached around the pockets of my jeans. Since today was such a rough day, I had never changed out of them. It only took seconds before I felt the medal object and pulled it out. With my other hand, I unleashed the blade from my pocket knife. Quickly, I stabbed the leg of the person behind me. Their grip loosened enough to give me some air. I pulled the knife out and stabbed them again but this time directly on their foot. My attacker released their grip and groaned in pain. In case I would need it again, I pulled the knife out and shot up without an ounce of hesitation. Without looking back I ran for my house. If I could make it then I could call the police.

My feet pounded against the ground. Whoever was behind me started to run in my direction. Their footsteps sounded far enough behind me that I could escape. The wind blew against me as I ran with all my might. For a brief moment, I was scared I wouldn't have the energy to get away after the restricted air flow.

The sound of the trees rustling got quieter with every second that I got closer to my house. I was no longer in the forest, and seconds away from reaching home. The door was practically right there. My toes hit a large rock which caused me to trip. The person behind tackled me the moment I got up.

Without any cushion except for the grass, my body smacked into the cold and unwelcoming ground with a large thump. The person turned me over so I was lying on my back. I raised my hand to stab them again, but they blocked it and stomped on my wrist with all of their strength. The knife fell from my hand. What I assumed to be a guy raised his fist and punched me once, and then again directly on my jaw. Blood filled my mouth along with something that was hard... possibly my tooth.

He grabbed the knife from the ground and stabbed it into my shoulder. I screamed. The warm blood ran down my skin, conflicting with the cold air. My heart pounded as the man wrapped the same rope around my neck and started to strangle me again. With my one free hand I tore the black, clothed mask from his face. He was not a man but rather a she.

Her eyes held no guilt or remorse as she tightened the rope. Instead, she smiled with such slyness and joy. I, on the other hand, felt great betrayal. The only reason I could make out Salem's face was because of the outside light. How could I have failed when I was so close to the door?

I needed to distract her if I wanted a fighting chance. I spit all the blood in my mouth directly onto Salem's face. She immediately looked disgusted and angry while she tried to wipe it off with one hand and keep hold of the rope with the other. Just then, I pulled the knife from my shoulder and stabbed it into her stomach. In a blink of an eye, Winston came into side view, lunging and clamping onto Salem's shoulder. He growled, thrashing his jaw as she screamed. Her body shook like a doll. Grounding herself, she raised her hand to stab him with the knife. Grabbing a near rock, I bashed it into her head.

She fell limp to the ground. Getting Winston inside, I locked all the doors and windows while calling the police. A loud bang interrupted while I was trying to explain everything to the operator. After a few seconds, the banging yielded to a crash. One of the windows had been broken. Salem's closed fist was bloodied with glass.

Salem climbed in, the sharp intact pieces cutting her open by the crown of her head. Winston began growling and barking viciously at Salem. Hearing Atlas's door loudly open, his footsteps were persistent as he ran down the stairs.

"Mom, what's happening?" His voice was nervous and shocked.

My shoulder throbbed along with my jaw. The dog barked and growled so loudly that I could barely hear myself think. He snarled, slobbering at the mouth. My best friend whom I had known for years was now trying to kill me. What was I supposed to do?

"Oh Julia, look at your son. It was difficult pretending not to see him but that is what he wanted me to do. Originally, the plan was that you would invite me in and feel so sorry for me that you would let me spend the night. While you were asleep, I was going to take the liberty of slitting your throat from ear to ear so that way the demon could have your soul. Of course, you just had to make things difficult and act out of character. If it wasn't for that boy coming back into your life then you wouldn't have reacted the way you did with me."

"You've been working with the demon this whole time?"

"No, Julia! Get it together. Must I explain everything to you all the time? Work implies that a salary comes with it but that's farthest from the truth. Everyone follows something. Science, their heart, a god, an average person, but I just so happen to follow and serve the demon. You see, he's using what you did to that boy as an excuse to torment you and take your soul. I was just going to be the supportive friend until he got you but then you and your son went off and weakened and angered him. So, he asked me to stop being on the sidelines. Oh, and Julia, before we go on why don't you get your dog out of here. If you don't, I might just snap his jaw. Second thought, I'll do it myself."

Salem dragged him by the skin on the back of his neck and tossed Winston outside before slamming the door shut. Salem walked over to me with ease as she picked up one of the kitchen knives from the block. Any fragment of life was void in her eyes.

"While I'm here, I'll have some fun with Atlas. Atlas, do you want to play a game? Looks like you used up all of your energy before. You should invest in some sleep if you want to ever protect your mother. Come on now, don't worry about it. I'm only going to do the same that you did to my friend. That way it'll all be fair."

"She can't hurt you right?" My sentence was rushed.

"If she's obtained power from the demon then she might be able too."

For the first time Atlas looked lost. Ignoring the pain from my shoulder I rushed up the stairs to Atlas and picked him up before Salem could get any closer and ran up to the bathroom. Without wasting a second I locked the door.

"Atlas love, look at me, okay?" His eyes were wide with worry.

"I can't let her hurt you. So you'll have to listen to me very carefully. Since she can hurt and see you, I need you to run and then hide. You're going to teleport out of this bathroom window and into the forest. You will run and hide. Whatever you hear, unless it's me trying to find you, don't come out."

"What are you going to do?" Atlas's eyes teared up as his voice broke.

"Shh, calm down. It's okay. I have my own plan alright? I'll be just fine. I need you to be brave for me though. I love you so much, okay?"

"I love you too, but promise me you'll come back and find me. Promise me that you won't get hurt. You can't leave me again. Why can't I stay and protect you!" I wiped the tears from his eyes.

"Atlas, you've protected me for a very long time, but it's time that I protect you instead. I won't ever leave you again. I promise. You have to go now though, okay?" Atlas tried to stop crying. I kissed him on his forehead and gave him a hug.

Chapter Fifteen

Parasite

ITHIN A FEW SECONDS HE was gone from my sight. I grabbed a can of old hairspray from under the sink and brought it in with me into the tub. Quietly, I stood behind the curtain. As expected, she banged violently on the door until it broke down.

"Julia, please, I know you and the boy are behind the curtain."

She grabbed the side and slowly opened it.

"Found you!" She said with a laugh.

I wasted no time and sprayed the hair spray into her eyes. She screamed and frantically rubbed her eyes. Next, I grabbed the curtain by the bottom and wrapped as much of her body in it that I could cover. She thrashed from one side to the other while I stepped out of the tub. My plan worked as her momentum carried both of us down with me on top, causing her head to smack off of the bathroom sink.

To my surprise, Salem got back. She tried to push me into the wall so I would let go of the curtain around her. My head crashed into the mirror, shattering it. Pain exploded through my skull. For a few seconds, my vision was blurry. But no matter how hard the hit, I refused to let go.

Mustering the tiny bit of strength remaining, I grabbed the lid from the toilet and smacked her in the head. The hit wasn't hard enough to kill her, but it was enough to knock her out before the cops got here. With a smack to the head and a splatter of blood from inside the shower curtain, her body fell limp as she crashed to the ground. Dragging her dead weight to the chair, I tied her to it with duct tape as best I could.

As I finished securing her right leg, Salem was starting to wake up. Quickly, I finished tying her up. She looked like she fell back to sleep.

"Julia." Salem breathed it out as though it would be her last words. With shaking hands, I checked the tape.

"Julia!" Her voice mimicked the demon's and my head snapped up only to discover Salem's face distorted.

Her eyes were completely black. Her face had become ghostly white, sunken in at her eye sockets and cheeks. Black veins protruded and pulsed throughout, especially around her eyes. She smiled only to reveal sharp razored teeth. This was not Salem. She lunged forward at me, effortlessly breaking through the duct tape. Her thumb dug into my knife wound. At that moment my front door opened.

"Darling, I came home early. At first I was going to stay at my friend's but I missed you and Atlas."

She froze immediately upon looking up and absorbing the gravity of the situation. Seizing the distraction to get Salem- or the demon off of me, I ran to get a knife and then shielded my mother. With a shaky hand, I brandished the knife at the demon using Salem as a vessel.

"Julia…"

"Mom, I love you but not now. There is no time for a family meeting to catch you up to speed."

The demon stood up straight and Salem's body became disformed. Her bones popped out of place, and her arms stretched to a great length along with her legs. What usto be Salem was now on all fours. Her legs and arms were about nine feet in length. Instead of her elbows being in the back of her arm they were forwards due to her arm being completely twisted around. Her jaw dropped two feet down as shrieking screams were produced from her mouth. The top of her head bent back completely so her mouth could become larger as rows of teeth presented themselves. A great demonic growl erupted from her or it.

"I don't have a plan for this." The words fell out of my mouth remembering the promises I made to Atlas.

Gripping my mother's hand I ran to the right which was the only place that could be narrowly avoided by Salem. With one hand the demon smacked me to the opposite side of the room where the crosses were. My back hit the wall with such force that all of the crosses toppled to the ground. Gasping for air, I tried to regain the wind that was knocked out of me.

Looking up, I saw that it wasn't going for me but instead for my mother. Using one hand, it knocked her down to the ground and proceeded to use both of her hands to hold her down. The sound of sirens filled the air from outside while the blue and red lights flashed through the windows onto the walls. Although hope ran through me, so did despair. How would I explain this to the police? What would they do when they saw this in front of them?

The demon stopped for a moment when he noticed the lights. While still holding my mother down, it returned to Salem's normal body form. From where I was, all I could see was a black, thick liquid being thrown up onto my mother. Salem got up while my mom wiped her face. Salem returned back to the middle of the living room and passed out.

"Mom!" I ran over to her. "Are you okay? What happened?"

"I don't know. I think I'm fine. Are you alright, Julia?" Her tone was flat and barely hinted of concern.

"Uhm, I… yeah, I just, I'm fine. Listen, when the cops ask what happened once you walked in you have to say that Salem was on top of me trying to harm me with the pocket knife and she got distracted when you walked in so I grabbed a knife and we tried to run upstairs. However, she caught up with us, threw me against the wall, I passed out, and then she went to attack you. When she heard the police, Salem tried to run out the front door and then I hit her with the handle of the knife, she fell and I asked you if you were okay, okay?"

"Okay."

The police barged in and I immediately began explaining what had happened. Many of them kept asking me the same questions over and over, separately interviewing me on the incident. They did the same thing with my mom. After what seemed like hours they finally left with Salem. I went back inside with my mother.

"Did you mention anything at all about the demon situation?"

"No, why would I ever do that?" She smiled widely.

"How about you go and get some rest mom."

"What will you do, Julia?"

"I have to go get Atlas and the dog."

She smiled and nodded. Carefully, she got up and walked up to her room, closing the door. After a few seconds standing there dumb founded, I went out of the house to go get my kid. Once I got close enough to the woods I could hear Atlas's desperate cries.

"Atlas, it's Mom. You can come out here now. Everything is okay now, I promise."

Atlas gave no response to me, so I was forced to go into the woods. At least Salem won't be there anymore. What if it's not even my son, rather the demon? Even my thoughts sounded exhausted from the situation. You know what? It's not like anything new can happen. My steps continued towards Atlas where I found him with Winston. The dog danced around him, winning to get the boy's attention.

"Atlas, are you okay?" His face turned to me covered in tears. His arms began reaching out to me. Immediately I hugged him and rubbed his back, telling him everything would be okay soon. Atlas's tears began to dampen my shoulder.

"Shhhh Atlas, you're okay. Do you want to go inside? I can get you warm tea, a blanket, and we could put on your favorite cartoon." Atlas pulled away from me while I wiped his tears.

"I thought I was going to lose you again. You were gone for so long! I started crying thinking about how you were gone. Mom, you scared me. You made me think you left me and I would never see you again. I couldn't lose you again. You're all I have! You're my mom!"

"Atlas, I know and I'm really sorry that I scared you but I'm here now. I love you okay? I won't ever leave you again. Please don't cry. I'm okay, you're okay."

"Then why is your shoulder hurt? Your energy is low and exhausted. Not to mention your jaw is all bruised. Your neck has strangle marks all around."

"Atlas, my heart is still beating and I'm with you here now, aren't I? I'm okay as long as you are as well. At the end of the day, we might be a little roughed up but as long as our minds are sane and we don't lose sight of what's important we're okay, plus a heartbeat but I'm sure you understand what I mean. I dismissed the ride in the ambulance to the hospital because mom used to be a nurse so she'll patch me up nicely until your energy is back to heal me."

"I'm glad you didn't just leave me here and go to the hospital?"

"I won't ever leave you again. You're my whole world."

Atlas needed to relax so we went inside and turned the television on. After I prepared a pot of tea for him and I, the cartoons played in the background. Soon enough he fell asleep under a blanket. Not before long, I did as well.

The clock from my room rang annoyingly throughout the house, showing no signs of letting up. Sluggishly, I got up from the couch and looked at Atlas's head which was awkwardly positioned due to the absence of a pillow. For a moment, I almost missed the soft gold light that was quickly retracting into his body. Tracing my fingers over the place I was once stabbed, I felt no pain or hole in the area. Could he heal me in his sleep? Putting those thoughts at bay, I grabbed a pillow. Carefully lifting his head, I slowly put it under him so as to not wake his tired body.

Turning to exit the room and go up the stairs, I saw my mother at the top of the stairwell, staring. Her eyes followed me while I walked up the stairway. My hand hovered over the polished wooden rail as I went up. I picked up my pace to pass my mother and turn off the alarm in my room. She did not take her eyes off of me.

Without looking back, I entered my room and hit the off button. It read 7a.m. I was late to work. Would it even be wise to be away from Atlas? He worries so much. Maybe he would like to go with me. A floorboard creaked behind me. Instinctively, my paranoid body turned around to face whatever demon might be awaiting. For whatever reason, my mother was directly behind me, so close that it would only take half a step to run into her.

"Oh my gosh! What is wrong with you? If I was any older you would have given me a heart attack!" I stepped back, bumping into my nightstand.

"Where are you going? Why don't you leave Atlas here. I wanted to take him out for some ice cream. Do you think he would enjoy such a thing, dear?" Her smile stretched to cover the entirety of her face.

"Actually, I was going to bring him into work." My gut screamed to take him with me.

"That's no place for a child, Julia, you can barely handle it yourself." Her tone was sharp with disbelief and assertiveness.

"Atlas can choose for himself."

She walked away to her room with fuming steps. Once I shook Atlas awake and asked him, he seemed excited at the idea. He teleported to the car before I could even begin to get ready. Listening to Atlas's impatient calls, I double checked for any bruises or cuts in the mirror that might be left. Thankfully, Atlas's magic healed them with what seemingly took no effort.

Once we arrived, Roman was at the front desk. He stood there, talking to the receptionist. Maybe I could convince her to type out that I arrived earlier than I actually did. The last thing I need is Mary trying to give me a three hour therapy session, interrogating me as to why I have been late so many times. Those were always annoying, not to mention a time waster.

"Hey, could you show me where storage room eight is?"

Mindlessly, I kept walking. After thinking about it I can ask her that once I get settled in. No sense in rushing when I know she will do it. At the end of the day, when I really get to thinking about it, if Mary were to find out she just might crucify me. Then again, I've done this several times. I'll just tell Mary the watered down truth of why I was late today.

"Should I take that as a no Julia?" My head snapped back at the faint sound of my name.

"Hmm? Sorry, I was lost in my thoughts."

"Could you show me where storage room eight is?" Roman looked at me with joy in his eyes and something else that I couldn't quite put my finger on as he stood there awaiting my answer.

Could I? Yes, but I really do have to get to Mary as soon as possible. If she takes three hours then that will only leave me with 15 minutes of prep time for Ezekial. Roman seems like the chatty type so then I would have no time to prep. Prepping is essential, I would have to stay after work. Punishment fits the crime, I guess.

"Sure, follow me." Holding back the reluctance in my voice, I smiled.

Looking at Atlas, I gave him an apologetic look. He just smiled at me, skipping down the hallway without a care in the world. Eventually, he got a little too far ahead for my comfort so I looked around to ensure that no one but Roman was around.

"Atlas, not too far away."

"Why?"

"The psych hospital isn't exactly a place for a kid."

"I'm a spirit though, so it cancels out the kid part."

"How old are you?"

"Seven…"

"Exactly, so get back over here, please."

"Okay" Atlas walked back over with boredom in his step.

"So, do you just fight demons everyday then?" Roman said it with a chuckle at the end.

"That's a light way of putting it. Not everyday though, it's just like he comes for a visit every now and then. You know, trying to take my soul. It's actually a really fun time. Sometimes, when we really miss him, we throw him a welcoming party. Would you like an invite to the next one? I really do think you'd enjoy it." Looking at him with seriousness, stifling a smile, I waited for an answer.

"Hm, I don't know about that one." Roman's tone only hinted of a slight joke.

"Why? You're nervous you might steal the spotlight? Don't worry about that he makes sure to make his presence known."

"Ah there you have it. I'm worried about being the center of attention. In all seriousness, how do you even sleep at night?"

"Melatonin, various sleeping pills, you know? Eventually, you get used to it. The things that once terrified you seem all so dull. For instance, in the event that I wake up to rapid footsteps or something falls on its own, a door slams shut, lights flickering, etc. all of those things become so normal." My face turned to Roman's wondering if he thought me to be crazy. If he did, he did nothing to give it away.

"If I didn't see it for myself, then I wouldn't have believed you."

"When I first met Atlas, I was about to admit myself into a psych ward. Never in my life did I think any of this existed. For days I felt like I was going insane. Luckily, Atlas was able to make a few things move in front of Salem. Look at that, we have arrived at storage room eight." My knuckles knocked against the door in order to prove my point. He said thank you as I started to walk away. It only took me several steps to turn back to him and stop.

"Oh and Roman, maybe be a bit careful when you go in there. Demons like to hang around in that storage room. You should be fine though. I only needed stitches after I escaped. Anyway, have a lovely day." I grabbed Atlas's hand and turned around to walk away.

"You're just kidding, right?" Roman sounded greatly concerned.

Instead of answering him I kept walking away and waved my hand in the air. The demon's only after me. He should be fine. I'll leave that up to his own interpretation. Atlas and I reached my office. He jumped into my swivel chair that was in front of the desk and started spinning. A knock sounded from my door. Atlas's spinning in the chair came to an abrupt stop.

Chapter Sixteen

Miscarriage of Justice

"Come in." Ezekial and a worker entered my office.

"Hello Ezekial, how are you doing?"

"Julia, or Dr. Bettington, You have to help me please! He's coming for me."

"What happened to you thinking that wasn't real?"

"I thought that maybe if I could get out someone could actually get rid of him like a priest or something, but he has no use for me now. He wants me gone. It'll be soon I know it. Dr. Bettington, you are my last resort. Please, help me. Save me! I know you know who I'm talking about. You must. Save me." Ezekial pulled on what little hair he had. His eyes pleaded with me like his life depended on me.

It doesn't matter now. I believed him and was connected to the very thing that he would talk so much about. Currently, there is no way that I could get him out even if I wanted to. Nobody would believe him, or me for that matter. I'm stuck. Ezekial is stuck. My fingers massaged my temples as I contemplated all of my possibilities that would lead to him getting out. None of them held any water. Guilt flooded me as I played the pretend game.

"Ezekial, nobody can hurt you here. Everyone in this facility wants to see you succeed. We will do everything in our power to make you feel safe. Do you want to talk more about this man?"

"Since I didn't complete my job, he is going to kill me."

"What was your job?"

"He needed me to hurt you beyond repair."

"At first, I tried scaring you so you might quit here and save yourself. Sadly, you stayed. None of that matters. I'll be gone. He'll have you and your boy." My professional tone became one of worry and fear of losing everything.

"What? What boy, Ezekial?" My voice was rushed as I leaned in to him.

"He's found a way to eliminate that obstacle of his."

"What do you mean eliminate?"

"Surely, an educated woman such as yourself would know that word. It's true that he has. I'll warn you about this much though. He's found a way, and you wouldn't ever expect it. Cherish the time you have now with that lovely son of yours, Julia. Time is running out. Mine just so happens to be sooner than yours, and the boy." As much as I wished to ask him questions, the least I could do is get him to think of the pleasant memories in life.

"What's your favorite meal?" Sadness weighed my soul.

"Beef curry, my father used to make the best of it. That was until he passed away. Have you ever tried the dish?"

"Unfortunately not, it sounds like a nice memory. Were you and your father especially close?"

"Yes, the best memories were when he would teach me how to repair old cars. It was a habit of his to buy them and fix it all up to its original beauty. My mother hated it. She would always nag him about how they had more important things to be spending money on. At one point it got so bad that my mother, well, she made him get a second job. She said that the only way he could keep up that hobby was if he got another job and solely used that money alone to do it. He did it. When he worked two jobs he'd come home late and begin his hobby. Even if it was three in the morning, I got up and worked on it with him in the garage we had."

"That sounds very sweet. I'm sure you gained a lot of knowledge doing such things."

"Truly, but if I can remember correctly then my father got me a dog about a year after I helped out with all of the cars. The dog's name was King. Looking back, I could have named him something better but I was young so it didn't really matter. King was a uhm, now what was he? Oh, that's right, a doberman. You see, my mother didn't like that either. She wasn't much of a dog person. No, she would have preferred a cat."

"Ezekial, I'm sorry." My apology was about something that I couldn't say out loud. I'm sorry that I'm leaving you all alone while you're struck with an incredulous fear. I'm sorry I'm keeping you here.

"Oh, don't worry about it. I'll be fine." Did he understand my deeper meaning?

Just then a worker said I was over the session about ten minutes. Why did it feel like I was sending a lamb to slaughter? Probably because I was. No, I am. We said our goodbyes.

"Don't worry about it, Mom. He's bluffing about me. Remember what I told you? I'm practically invincible." Once again, that word practically hung in the air for better or worse. Staring into Atlas's eyes, I caught the uncertainty that hid behind a large rock of bravery.

"Your grandma was right. I'm sorry that I brought you here."

"Don't be!" He gave me a cheerful smile to reassure my worried mind.

Practically is the part that I worried about. That word gave a hint that under the right conditions something could be possible. My hands cradled my head while I thought about how if Ezekial died tonight, that would be my fault. He's not a bad man, he's not even crazy. Everything he said about Atlas was also too much. What did he mean? I would rather die than lose my son, again.

"Mom?"

"Yeah?"

"Are you okay?"

"Of course I am. Atlas, I have to meet with my boss for a while. I won't force you to stay. If you would like to teleport home then go ahead."

Atlas did exactly that. Once I got down to Mary's office, I walked in and sat down. Her room was painted a soft yellow. To me, yellow wasn't a good color for any room, but that was her favorite. Mary's desk was chipped and wooden. Even her chair looked like it needed to be replaced. She leaned back into her chair and crossed her arms.

"Listen Julia, I like you. I do. You're a good worker and a joyful presence in this gloomy workplace. However, it is a workplace. You can't show up late like this. Once is understandable but Julia, you've done it five times this month. There has to be something more going on because I can't honestly believe a good person like you would do such a thing without any reason."

I just want to go home, and be with my family. Who is she to lecture me on professionalism in the workplace? Mary is the one who covers everything up. She probably just wishes for someone to confide in her. Mary loves giving out advice. My boss is kind, but I don't have the energy for this.

"Mary, to be frank with you my best friend, or ex-best friend tried to kill me last night and almost succeeded. Luckily the cops came in at the right time before she could finish my mother and I off. Not to mention my mother. She recently came back into my life after a seven years absence. Five months ago my nephew started staying with me. His name is Atlas."

"Oh, so, uhm, that's why Salem isn't here today, or answering her phone." Mary looked dumbfounded.

Behind her, on her soft yellow walls, was a red liquid that started to stream down like syrup. The demon appeared next to it heaving. His body hunched due to the room being too small. The demon smiled, corners of his mouth reaching all the way to where his ears were supposed to be if he had any. His skin was burnt as usual.

"One" His voice boomed as he took a step forward to Mary. The lights flickered in the room.

"Two" The demon grabbed Mary by her hair and snapped her head back.

"Three" Using his nails he slit her throat all the way across. Blood came pouring out from her neck.

The desk flew to the opposite side of the room and smacked into the wall breaking entirely. Mary's body slumped out of the chair and fell onto the floor creating a thump as the light left her eyes. The color drained from her skin. The demon practically ran towards me as I sat there, wide eyed, frozen, and with my mouth open in astonishment. My body felt like cement filled every cell. No matter how much I tried to move, or even scream it was as though I was paralyzed and my voice was no longer available to me.

"JULIA!" Mary's hands were waving in front of my face as she stood instead of sitting in her chair.

"Uhm yes?" The sound of my tone revealed nothing but uncertainty and confusion.

"What happened? You just went wide-eyed, mouth was open, and you were even crying." Her concerned eyes peered into mine.

"Crying?" My fingers brushed at my eyes only to wipe a wet substance away from my face.

"Julia, how about you get home and get some rest."

Slowly, I got up from my chair and walked out. Maybe I should just wait until I go home and catch my breath. I'll rest in my office. Instead of sitting down at my chair, my body essentially fell into the comfortable couch typically used for my patients. A knock sounded at the door. Maybe if I don't answer they will go away.

"Hello? Julia are you there? Could we talk for a second?" Roman called.

Now isn't the time. I'm terribly tired. What if it's work related?

"Come in" He opened the door and stood near my desk with his hands in his pockets.

"Please don't take this the wrong way but I won't be a victim to your demon, right?"

"Roman, I don't think you're going to be dragged into this again."

"What will you do about it? I mean, you have a plan to get rid of it, right?"

"No. I don't have a plan to get rid of it, let alone save my soul. There is nothing that I know to do that would fix my problem. I don't know how to protect my son, my mother or even me for that matter. If I knew I wouldn't be in this situation. My friend tried to kill me, a patient of mine shouldn't even be a patient, I'm tired, and feel like I'm going insane. So, if you are asking me if there is any way shape or form you will get dragged into this then in all honesty just don't bother with me because from what I gathered it only goes after the people who I'm involved with."

"Wait, your friend tried to kill you?" There it was, the shock in his tone.

"Yes, last night, all of it just collided with no warning." Peering at him to see if he was slowly inching towards the door, I wondered why he hadn't left yet.

"Why are you here? Shouldn't you be at home or talking to the police?"

"Yeah, no, I was up all night talking to them and only got three hours of sleep before I came here with Atlas."

"Where is he by the way?"

"At home. He didn't want to stay any longer. He probably missed the dog."

"Well Jules, I have to get home but you should too. Get some rest. Don't beat yourself up too badly. You'll figure this out because you're smart." The words were said with his heart, not just to close the conversation.

"You too. Have a good night as well. You ought to considering it's demon free."

Roman walked out the door. After that, I decided to pack up and go home. As I was about to turn off the light and walk out my door, a creak came from the corner of my room. Nothing could be seen standing there.

"Screw off." Immediately after saying it my hand shot up to cover my mouth as I stood there in astonishment from my own words. Never in the time of my existence did I think I would dare to say screw off to a demon that had the power to kill me at any given second.

Upon saying those two words, I got out of the room as quickly as possible. Leaving the place gave me a false sense of security. Right as I neared the front doors to leave, the hallway light flicked off and then on. My breath hit the window door creating a fog. Fear ran through my veins as an overwhelming coldness flooded the air around me. I turned around to see whatever awaited me.

"Atlas?" His figure stood at the end of the hall. My voice cracked as I said his name. My fear compromising the ability to speak.

"Atlas, please answer me. ATLAS!" Every atom within my body screamed to me that it was not my child.

He smiled widely like he usually did, showing off his dimples. The light stopped flickering momentarily. Atlas's small body began to deteriorate as his skin melted from his bones, onto the tiled grey floor. His eyes started to push out from his sockets and droop down his face.

"Mom! Mommy help me!" Atlas cried and wailed in dreadfully agonizing pain. His body lit up on blue fire as I ran to him.

Once I reached his body, his bones started to pop from what little skin he had left and the demon came out from him, slowly stretching to his full size. As though time slowed all around me, I couldn't get up as fast as normal. I could hear myself slowly breathing in rhythm with my erratic heartbeat. It took me everything, but I was able to get on my feet and start running towards the door as fast as I could.

I heard a metal clanking behind me. Only a few seconds after that, a metal chain unforgivingly wrapped around my neck, snapping me back to the floor. The demon dragged me back with the cold chain wrapped tightly against my neck. For the second time, I frantically grabbed and pulled at the chain that threatened to take my life away. The repetitive attack felt like payback for my chain wrap around his throat. While my feet kicked against the tiled floor, hot tears escaped from my eyes. With each passing second, my breathing became more desperate and labored. This was not a human that I could fight off. This was a demon that planned to haunt me until it got exactly what it wanted from me. No matter the way, he will kill me.

Black dots spotted my vision as the strength left my body. The grip on the chain that wrapped around my neck loosened. Finally, the demon reached a room and raised the chain up to where I was in the air. He threw me inside while I rolled on the floor. My hip bones found the rough surface first. Despite my vision failing me, I was able to tell it was my office. The chain no longer tightened around my neck. However, the feeling of coming close to passing out lingered. The demon walked over to me and pulled my head up to his face by my hair.

"I'll take your boy from you, Julia. God won't be able to do anything about it either. Even He understands the order. Everything you and that boy did to me will be inflicted upon you both. If you played nice, it would only be you. You just can't help making others miserable. Can you?"

The demon wrapped his hand tighter around my hair and slammed my head down.

Chapter Seventeen
Drowning in Insanity

"Julia? Hey, Julia wake up!"

My head pounded violently as I opened my eyes. Someone was shaking me lightly. Their hands gently held onto my shoulders. When I opened my blurry eyes, Salem's black veined filled face was in front of me. She opened her mouth and let out a demonic shriek. A scream escaped from my lips while I pushed her away with all the strength I could gather, sitting up. Only then was it that my vision cleared.

"Oh my gosh Roman I am so sorry!" He looked at me with surprise.

"Are you okay?" Roman's voice sounded hesitant and worried.

"I, I thought you were someone else. Did I hurt you?"

"No, but uh, do you need me to call someone? You're bruised up really bad, Jules."

"Julia, not Jules, but no. Why are you here so late?"

"Late? It's six in the morning when my shift starts. What happened to you?"

"Mr. Spawn of Satan decided to pay me a visit on my way out. Is that my phone?" Examining my hands, I caught bruises all over them.

"Yes, I found it by the front doors when I came in. That's why I checked for you here. Are you sure you're okay?"

"Other than severe brain trauma I think I'm okay." My hand rubbed against my forehead in an attempt to soothe my pounding head.

"Seriously?" His tone gave away the fact that no matter what I said, I was extremely short of convincing him otherwise.

"Yeah, but it's nothing I won't be able to handle. Thank you for bringing my phone and coming to check on me. Sorry, if I've kept you from your work. Who is training you now that Salem is gone?"

"Some guy named Robin, but I think he is out today. I'm thinking of just floating around. Everyone here seems too busy to train me."

"Busy? Only few people actually do anything. In any other psych hospital, you would have people running around, busy all of the time but not here. Every other place has people doing their jobs like they should. Or at least the ones I've been too. Mary is lucky we haven't gotten shut down yet. So, the only time anyone here is too busy for someone is when something happens. Do you know anything?"

"No, but let me help you up." His voice signaled that he could care less what was going on with everyone else.

Roman stood up and held out his hand for me to grab. As I got up a wave of dizziness hit me. How was I supposed to work like this? Roman caught me the moment my mind began slipping from consciousness. His hands cautiously held me before I could fall to the cold floor. Without letting go, Roman guided me to the couch in my office. All I could think about was the pain that invaded my head. This would be the second time my head was harshly slammed against something. Internally groaning, I thought about the missed calls and texts I would have from my mother and Atlas. Immediately upon thinking about the notion, I reached for my phone and looked at the lock screen. twelve missed calls from my mother and twenty messages. Each message was made clear that I needed to get home.

Sending a false text about me having to work overtime and deciding to spend the night in my office, I sighed in relief to her reply of understanding. Although it was not the truth, there was no chance that I would burden her with unnecessary worry. Surely, I'll be fine.

"Roman, since you said you weren't busy do you think that maybe you could help me with organizing old paper work? It's just that I have so many calls to make. Please don't feel obligated."

"Yeah, sure." With a smile on his face and a skip in his voice, I felt at ease.

Roman was about to say something else, but Mary knocked on my door. She looked especially troubled. Worry was carved into her face as though she carried a thousand burdens on her back. Mary was… emotional when it came to everyday life problems. I guess you could describe her as a very empathetic person. That sounded much better than emotional. Perhaps she got up and her dog ran away again. For whatever reason she always would vent to me about things like this.

"Julia, come to my office for a bit. We need to talk."

"Absolutely." Her tone was very formal. Thoughts of me getting fired began to flood my mind.

Shoving my anxiety down, Roman and I exchanged a look of mutual understanding. Both he and I felt like Mary's tone was too formal for it to be about anything good. She was always such a friendly, joking type of person. Keeping a respectable distance from Mary while we walked to her office, I pondered in my mind all the what if's that could begin to unfold in front of me in these coming minutes. Not a single one of them had a good outcome. We sat down in her office.

"Julia, you may have noticed that the workers are unusually busy today. That has to do with what I need to talk to you about. Please brace yourself. I'm very sorry to relay this news to you. Upon one of the workers doing rounds today, they found Ezekial suffering from a severe heart attack. Unfortunately, he didn't make it." Her eyes were filled with sorrow.

"No, Ezekial was supposed to be the one of the ones that got out. He wasn't supposed to die here. He wasn't a bad man. Ezekial wasn't supposed to stay locked up here. He should have gotten out and lived a normal life. Dying here isn't what he deserved. Mary, he was so close to leaving. All I needed was some more time."

"Julia, I'm really sorry. I know that he was one of the few patients that you could imagine a future for outside of these walls. However, I'm sure that you did everything you could to try to help him. Ezekial had a very serious mental illness. The time that it would have taken him to get out of here couldn't have been shortened."

"So, am I just supposed to accept that? It's my job to get people like him out of here."

"It's your job to make their lives better, Julia. Getting them out isn't always a guarantee. That takes a lot of time. Don't blame yourself. Listen, I know you're upset about this but due to how understaffed we are, especially now, I can't let you take leave for this or even go home early."

"It's fine, Mary. They teach us in school how to disassociate ourselves from our patients in times like this. Have a good day." Without waiting for her reply, I shot up from the uncomfortable chair and walked out the door.

Why? That poor man just wanted to get out and try to save himself. It was my selfishness that prevented such a basic need. If only I had just gotten him out into the real world. It sucks all the more that I have to go back in there with Roman and act like everything is well. Before I opened my office door, I took a deep breath.

"What was that all about? It seemed like she was going to fire you."

I slumped down into my office chair as I pulled some medicine for my head out from the drawer. A tired sigh escaped me just as I was about to take the pill. For a moment, I just looked at Roman. Maybe if I went into work with his attitude things wouldn't be so dreary. It was stupid and naive of me to think that with my degree I could save lives. Instead, I ended up ruining one. A heart attack? At his age? Sure, he had mental problems, but with what he told me about the demon coming to get him? The whole thing is too coincidental.

"Uhm, Yeah I thought so too. A part of me would prefer that over what happened. Ezekial, a patient of mine, died this morning. That's why everyone is so busy. Robin must be scrambling right now. There is another patient that was to come in today. He was assigned to handle that. However, he is also the only one to get Ezekial's family lined up with everything. It's a whole process."

"I'm really sorry." His words held weight. If I was going to cheer up in any sense, I needed to resume a normal conversation.

"Me too. So, Roman did you figure out the way I wanted the files to be organized from the notes?"

"Of course I did. I know that you killed Ezekial. What a bitch move. That's why you deserve to burn in hell. You could have gotten him out."

My head snapped up at this.

"What did you say?"

"I said that I understood how to organize the files. Also that your necklace is cool. Where did you get it?"

"Sorry, I thought you said something else. My father gave it to me when I was eight. He got it when he went to South Dakota for a trip. When he came back, he gave it to me."

My fingers played with the golden necklace that was in the shape of an eternal sign with stars that hung from it in the middle of the symbol. For the first few years that I had it, I kept it tucked away. Then suddenly, one morning, I decided to put it on and I've worn it ever since.

"Julia, do you not have any patients today?" He looked at me with curiosity in his eyes.

"No, I do but my next one isn't until 2:30."

"Your job seems really draining. I don't think I could do it."

"Julia!" The demon's loud, strangled voice boomed right next to my ear.

"Stop it!" My voice sounded more terrified than I intended as I shot up from my desk chair and covered my ears. Despite my ears ringing from the loud noise, I uncovered them.

"Maybe you're the one that needs to be seen instead of your patients." Roman let out an uncomfortable laugh. "Are you okay?"

"I'm going insane." Looking around the room, I felt a deep uneasiness settle inside my heart.

"I would agree with you if I never saw the demon, however, that image is now forever haunting me. Have you thought about doing an exorcism?"

"How would one even go about doing that?"

"I'm not for sure but it always works in those horror movies."

"True, maybe I should start investigating my options."

"Calling the ghostbusters is also a very reliable option. Maybe I could put in a good word for you and they'll give you a discount, Jules."

Roman and I laughed for a moment and then proceeded to joke for the remaining hours until 2:15 hit. Even though Roman's presence caused me to get practically nothing done, the humor was something that I desperately needed. He really did surprise me. Instead of labeling me as crazy, which would have been much easier to accept than reality, he tried to begin a friendship. Maybe the whole demon thing just intrigues him more than anything else. Either way, he brought a sense of humor with him.

"Hey Roman, it's almost time for me to see my patient and I have to prep in the meantime so..."

"Alrighty then, I'll call the ghostbusters while you're busy."

"Please do. See you later." We exchanged smiles and a laugh as he left.

"Bye, Jules."

"Julia!" I yelled out to him trying to correct his mistake. Unfortunately he left the room before I even started saying it. I'm positive he still heard me. Once I finished with my patient's session, I stayed for a couple more hours and then went to leave.

The walk to the front doors seemingly took longer than ever before. With each step, my heart beat a little faster and my hands shook a little more. Each time I played the memory of last night in my head, my pace picked up just slightly. Although I was walking out of the building, away from the possible danger, it only felt like I was marching to my death. No matter how much I thought about it, I couldn't escape the feeling of dread.

On the way home, I sped on the bumpy roads. Praying, a rare occurrence for me, that maybe I wouldn't die and although I didn't feel like I deserved it, that I would somehow in all this screwed up mess get a happy ending. Happy endings were only in fairy tales. No matter the circumstance reality is reality I thought. Why would God care to save me?

Helplessly drowning in my own thoughts, driving was at the very bottom of my main focus. The demons seemed to be getting so impatient. Impatient to succeed while I suffered a devastating loss. I felt like a fool that was wasting every second of my time not being locked in a room and trying my best to find a solution. I needed a solution that would ensure the safety and happiness of my Atlas, mother, and I. A part of me hoped that somehow in this long equation Roman would be involved.

Soon enough, my time will run out and when it does the real question is will I have a bullet proof plan to save everyone within my path, or will I be stuck clueless just as I am now? Each and every one of my thoughts felt so useless. Mom always taught me as a child that actions spoke louder than words. Except, now, I didn't have words to speak or actions to execute. Only thoughts that helped no one and solved nothing.

My thoughts overwhelmed me as a sense of helplessness mixed in with a massive self pity party that only brought me down. Is saving what I have now even possible? I feel like I'm retreating when I should be attacking.

"Shit!"

My car came to a loud ear piercing stop as I turned my wheel trying to avoid what lay in front of my car. The wheels screeched in protest against the road, spinning around for a few seconds and finally coming to a stop. Paying no mind to the pain in my stomach from the seatbelt, I put my car in park and stepped out. My body shook in reaction to the situation. Looking around, I noticed that the deer was nowhere in sight nor was there any damage to my car. I concluded that I avoided hitting the deer completely like I had hoped. A shaky sigh came out of me, releasing the anxiety that was produced from the scene.

Getting back in, I started on the road again, this time, refusing to get lost in my thoughts that threatened to take me down. Like I should have in the first place, I kept all of my focus on the road. It wasn't long before that I reached home. Looking up from inside my car, I saw that my mother stood in a window on the top floor, barely illuminated. Awkwardly waving to her, she gave no response to me back.

CHAPTER EIGHTEEN
NARROWLY AVOIDED

"MOM! I MISSED YOU SO much! I wanted to see you at work but Grandma said that you would be really busy so it would be best to stay here at home. Are you hungry? I made you a sandwich." Atlas's tone was bright and cheerful.

"You made me dinner? That's so sweet of you! I'm sure that it's the best sandwich in the world. What flavor is it?"

"Peanut Butter, your favorite." He looked at me with joy in his eyes as his dimpled smile showed through his small face.

"Good thing you made it for me. I was just about to pass out from lack of energy." I ruffled his red curly hair as I walked over to the table to eat what he had prepared.

"Yeah, your energy level seems really low actually. Did something happen to you?"

"Just a normal work day. What did you do today?" Thankfully, I covered up the bruises with the makeup in my car. I didn't dare to worry the little boy any more than need be, nor use his energy. Those bruises could heal on their own.

"Nothing really, I went and played with Winston. Are you positive nothing is wrong?"

"Nope. Everything is perfect love."

"Sure. WIll you be gone all day tomorrow?" His tone was no longer happy but hinted of sadness and loss. Atlas stared off absent minded at the television. I got up and walked over to him.

"I shouldn't be. Yesterday was a fluke."

"Whatever happened to the Roman guy? Has he freaked out a whole bunch since?" Atlas's face held a knowing amusement.

"No, surprisingly not. I guess he took it a whole lot better than I did. He does seem rather curious."

"You should invite Roman over for dinner tomorrow. That way he can ask a bunch of questions. Don't worry, I can answer them all." Atlas shot a thumbs up to me.

"Uhm, I don't think Roman and I are that close of friends for me to invite him over for dinner. Chances are he would be uncomfortable."

"Mom, he deserves to know since he had to go through it. Besides, you said he was curious. Oh, and trust me on one thing, he won't be uncomfortable. Just invite him over." Atlas winked at me along with his dimpled smile. Ignoring whatever his wink meant, I decided to negotiate.

"Okay, but under one condition. You have to last two full minutes of being tickled."

"You'll never catch me alive!" Atlas laughed and quickly got off the couch running up the stairs.

His footsteps sounded rushed as he tried to get up the flight of stairs faster than I could. Atlas's innocent giggles echoed throughout the hall. He got up to the top and rounded a corner. Hearing him slam a door, I searched a few rooms. Feeling a sense of victory, I found him in the spare bedroom. Before I could get to him, he ran out and back down the stairs. It didn't take but a few seconds for me to capture him.

I started to tickle him as his laughs filled the room. Ensuring him a fair deal, I counted out loud over his echoing giggles. Atlas kept laughing uncontrollably until I reached the two minute mark and stopped. This meant he won since he didn't teleport away within the time frame.

"Darn it, you won!" Smiling at him, I admitted defeat.

"Thank you, it was very difficult. Now that you have accepted your defeat you have to make sure that Roman comes over for dinner." Atlas looked sly due to his winning.

"I'll invite him. Why don't you go to bed? It's getting late."

"I'm not tired though. Plus! I don't need to sleep since I'm a ghost."

"Yeah, but, I'll be going to bed and I don't feel comfortable with you roaming around the house with everything going on if I'm not around. Besides, sleep gives you magic energy."

"Grandma's awake." His eyes held great pride as he thought he found a loophole.

"No, Grandma is going to sleep soon as well." I shook my head as reassurance that I wasn't going to budge.

"Please!" He pouted with his hands clasped together.

"Atlas, I'm telling you to go to bed."

"Okay."

He let out a sigh of defeat and slowly went up the steps, looking back every now and then. When he did make it to his room, I put a pot of tea on and then went up to tuck him in. Leaving him, I knocked on my mother's bedroom door. The sound of my knuckles hitting on the door produced a shuffling of footsteps from the opposite side.

"What do you want, Julia?" She swung open the door at a speed suggesting she was angry.

"I just wanted to let you know that we'll probably be having a guest over for dinner tomorrow." Her face went from blank to a wide smile within a split second. She made a habit of doing that lately.

"Oh, dear, thank you for telling me. I'll stay in my room."

"Really?" Surprise fought its way in my tone.

"Yes really. I'm not at your damn beck and call for every social dinner you have." She was livid.

"Why are you cursing at me? It's not like I was being harsh with you."

"Sometimes Julia you just get on my nerves. Leave me alone now, I need my sleep for these old bones."

The tea whistled impatiently for me to pour it. Going back downstairs to the blackness that filled the rooms, I realized that I left the lights on, not off. However there was one light which was the blue flaming fire that continued to make the pot of tea whistle. The teapot's whistle grew louder with each moment's hesitation. I'll be fine, I thought.

My hand grazed the smooth railing, giving me a sense of comfort as I went back downstairs. Reaching the lights, I turned them on. Everything seemed alright. Pouring a cup of tea and going back upstairs, I looked over my shoulder every few seconds just to ensure that nothing was sneaking up on me. My skin crawled with insecurity at the unknown.

Making it down the hallway and to my bedroom, I closed the door and got in bed. Reaching for the melatonin from my nightstand, I took two instead of one. A shadow of doubt hung around me when I thought about being able to have a complete night's rest. What a dream that would be. If only, I could achieve such a thing.

As I finished my tea and curled myself further under the blankets, my eyelids began to feel like stone as they weighed themselves down. Only then did my loud mind quiet to nothing, and all of my anxiety was released with each time that I exhaled.

"Julia, wake up." My mother's voice sounded loud but not as loud as the baby that was crying in the background. Usually, I would be groggy and tired; but at the sound of a baby crying loudly my mind was forced into thinking clearly.

"How come you have him?" I sat up at the sight of her carrying my baby wrapped in a red satin blanket. The child slept peacefully in the warmth of her arms.

"Get up so you can see Atlas's cleansing ceremony."

"Ceremony? Give him to me please."

"Oh, I can't believe you aren't up for it either. You're over here sleeping. It was me that had to answer to the crying of your child! Atlas doesn't have the time for this. Neither do you. Come out in your pajamas or so help me I'll drag you out." She looked at me with absolute hatred behind her eyes.

Holding him in one arm, she grabbed me with the other. That would surely leave a bruise. Eventually, she let go and used her other hand to get me up as she completely let go of my child. Quickly, I sat up and caught him mid air. My heart pounded in fear that if it wasn't for me catching him he could have easily gotten seriously hurt. He is only six weeks old.

"What is wrong with you mom! You just about hurt Atlas!"

"You're the one who hurt him. Follow me."

Mom walked out of my room and all the way to the front door. Twenty people circled an enormous fire in the front yard. Atlas let out a sudden wail. His grey eyes sparkled with hints of golden specks. When I realized how cold it was, I took my robe and wrapped it around him. Pulling him closer to my chest as to warm him further, I rocked him ever so slightly. The dampness of the grass wet my feet with each step that I took.

"If you keep doing that, you'll spoil him." Mom looked at me accusingly. Rolling my eyes at her, I continued with the question that popped into my mind.

"Who are all these people?" Worry started to fill my voice.

"Friends" I stopped walking at her answer. My mother instinct kicked and screamed for me to run away as I looked into the people's faces. I looked up at the sky to gather an estimate of what time it might be. The light of day was just barely breaking into the crevices of the sky. Friends or not the people who gathered here needed to leave immediately.

"Tell your friends to leave. I'm going inside." The fire crackled in the background as it grew larger upon the second. Without a delay, mom yanked my arm and spun me around so fast that I fell to the ground, almost dropping my son. Atlas wailed out in response to the sudden movement.

"You spoiled brat! What do I have to do to get you to listen to me? Look, you're upsetting the poor baby. Let me help him." Her face softened as she stared at my child.

She reached out to grab him, but I stepped back. A few of her friends approached me with wide smiles from ear to ear on their faces, barely illuminated by the light from the fire. They grabbed my arms as my mother pried Atlas from me. His cries filled the air and broke my heart. While he unclenched his hands, the smallest golden light shined through.

"Give me my son back right now!" Rage filled me as she cooed at him.

While I tried to fight off the people who restrained me, my mother walked closer to the fire. It sickened me as she smiled at my baby so sweetly. The people dragged me closer to the fire. Every one of them started to smile at me. Half of them began to chant something in a foreign language.

"Julia, your son is so beautiful! You truly did a good job. Oh, he is so cold. You should have really dressed him more warmly. It is his ceremony, after all." She raised Atlas up in the air and showed him to all the people. "My friends, this is my grandson, who was birthed by Julia. After six long weeks, we can finally have the ceremony we've been preparing for years. Julia's excitement has been lacking, unfortunately. Now let us offer the sacrifice that we've been waiting to give for so long. Friends, if we allow this child to grow any older, we will not be able to sacrifice Julia. It's powers will protect her with his love. We need Julia's soul. He needs her soul. Atlas would only block him. Instead of letting this child live and protect her with his pure love and power, we must terminate him. This is a sad night, but the Man up above has sent Atlas to protect Julia! We will not stand for such a thing! We refuse to let God have his way!"

The flames danced dangerously close to Atlas as she brought him down from the air. He screamed and cried with all his might. His tiny hands and legs kicked with all of their strength. Flicks of gold illuminated in his tiny palms. It was the fire light that allowed me to see the tears that streamed down his small face.

"Get him away from the fire! Mom! I said get him away from the fire!" She stepped back and calmed Atlas from crying. She then gave him a kiss on his forehead, and in the same motion, threw him into the roaring flames.

"Atlas!" I screamed at the top of my lungs for my baby boy. The strangers let go of me as I ran towards the fire. My body collapsed next to it as I sobbed from the gaping hole that had just been torn in my heart. Rocking myself back and forth, I cried.

"Atlas! No, my baby boy. Please! You killed my baby boy! Oh my poor baby boy. You took him from me!"

My mother leaned down to me with a furious look on her face. She grabbed my chin and snapped my tear stained face towards her. At first, she smiled but then anger crept back into her expression.

"You are next, Julia. Do you feel that pain? Now imagine it twenty times worse. Imagine feeling it for an eternity." She leaned up and away from me. "Alright, now for the less pure sacrifice. Put the mother in." They grabbed me and threw me in the fire. Searing pain ran through me as the flames burned me.

"Atlas!" Waking up from a sweat I wasted no time running to Atlas's room where I found my mother standing over him. Her hand reaching for his face. My love's door slammed shut before I could enter. Twisting the knob frantically, I stepped away from the locked barrier and slammed myself into it, breaking open on the second try.

"What are you doing?" Upon hearing my voice Atlas woke up.

"Mom?" He sounded confused and nervous.

"Julia dear, you sound so nervous. I'm sorry if I frightened you. I heard you screaming Atlas's name and so I thought something might be wrong with him."

"I had a nightmare."

"Well are you alright now? Did you ever think that maybe it wasn't a nightmare. If you had him, that's what would have happened." Mom had a smirk carved into her face. As she replied her voice slowly transitioned to the demon's.

"What the hell?" My alarmed voice cracked from my throat.

"Don't you dare curse at me, Julia! All I did was ask if you were okay!"

"I'm fine. Atlas, come here. You're going to sleep with me tonight." Atlas tiredly grabbed my open hand as I pulled him towards my room. Turning around, I caught daggers in my mother's stare. She watched longingly until we closed the door. My son crawled in bed before I locked the bedroom door, refusing to fall asleep. Her footsteps echoed towards my room while I held Atlas under the covers. His exhausted body was already asleep as the shadows of her feet crept under the doorway stretching inside. My mother's hand clasped the doorknob rattling it in anger until she finally gave up. Three times she tapped her nail against the wooden door dragging it down to produce a scratching noise, letting out a darkly low chuckle only to walk away.

CHAPTER NINETEEN

LOST IN THE FIRE

———◆———

"**A**TLAS, SET THE TABLE WILL you?"

"Sure, I think that Roman is a little late." Atlas's tone hinted that Roman was being a bad guest.

"Only by ten minutes. I don't really think someone is late until they arrive 15 minutes after the agreed time."

"No, I think someone is late when they don't arrive on the agreed time." Atlas shook his head as he spoke those words. Silently, I disagreed with him.

"Oh, look at that! It must be him knocking on the door."

Today would be the day that Roman gets to come and explore the world of demons. Not that I know anything really of it myself. What if he thinks badly of Atlas, as though he isn't a kid? He is one. Stuffing my worries down, I opened my door.

"Roman! Come in."

"Thank you, but are you trying to kill me? It's just that you drag me out into the middle of nowhere. Forest, old creepy house, away from civilization and all. It's kind of hard not to expect you to kill me, Jules."

"Darn it, you got my secret plan! Well, now I'll have to go with plan B."

"Spooky, what might that be?"

"That would spoil the surprise. Julia by the way."

"Hey, kid. It's Atlas, right?" Roman gave my child a cheerful smile that relieved any anxiety of the negative presumptions I thought he might have of Atlas.

"Yeah, if you have any questions about the whole demon thing then I'm all ears." Atlas shrugged at the end of his sentence, letting off a coolness.

Roman kept conversation with Atlas for a while. My thoughts happily decided to run wild. What if I end up dragging Roman into my mess by inviting him over here? For whatever reason, the demon spared him that once, or at least until he tried to intervene. Just because I lost a friend does not mean I have a right to get another one and in return screw their lives up. What if I can't defeat this demon and then it moves on to him? No, that would be so morally wrong to knowingly plague another person with an evil entity.

However, I did warn him that as long as he keeps away from me, nothing will happen to him. No, that still isn't right. Everyone has free will to do what they want so it's not like I can stop him from becoming a part of my life. Then again, I can choose and limit who my situation affects. I could really go on and on about this, going back and forth, but it is necessary to make the final decision in order to lessen the damage. Either way, I had to pick my poison.

"Whatever you might be thinking about it would be a good idea to stay focused before your finger hits that boiling water. How do you not feel the heat from it?" Roman's concerned voice chimed in.

"Hmm? Oh, yeah that would be a good idea. Just caught in my thoughts."

"You do that a lot." His voice alluded that he would like to hear about those thoughts. However, I wasn't fond of that idea.

"Hard not to when there is a lot going on, you know?"

"Do you need any help with dinner?"

"Oh, no, please, you're a guest. Just relax." I gave him a smile before carrying on.

"Unfortunately, I can't relax if I'm worried about you burning yourself while lost in your thoughts."

"If you truly don't mind then it would be helpful for you to take the food out the oven."

"Will do. What were you thinking about?" Well, I guess he won't give up.

"Uhm, I just, I guess I feel like I'm dragging you into my mess and I don't like the feeling of risking that for another human being. It feels criminal. To be quite frank, I think that the risk of you suffering a great devastation is too high for comfort. Please don't take that as an indication of me not liking you, or not enjoying the company but it just, it's too high."

"Jules, it's worth the risk. If it makes everyone feel better, I'll keep a respectable distance." Now that tone was filled with something that I couldn't quite put my finger on. Regardless, it was extraordinarily heartfelt.

"What is?" Standing there clueless, I waited for his answer.

Roman just smiled at me and shook his head. What did he mean? Despite what he may think his life is not worth risking. See, now I'm going to be up thinking about this. Wait, did he say Jules instead of Julia again?

You know what that's really not on the top of my concerns. I felt Atlas tug on my shirt.

"Atlas, I love you to death but instead of pulling on my shirt could you say my name?"

"I did, I said Mom, is dinner done?"

"Sorry, I didn't hear you. It is finished. I'll fix your plate. Go sit down, okay?"

Once we all sat down at the table and began eating Roman paused for a bit and just stared at Atlas. After Roman glanced at him a couple times, and didn't look away, Atlas finally spoke up. The expression covering his face hinted he was going to try and be clever.

"What, you've never seen a ghost before?" Atlas smiled before he went back to eating.

"Sorry, I just never expected ghosts to eat."

"Spirits can eat if they want to, not that they have to."

Once Roman finished with all of his questions, he helped me clean up. Next, we all watched a movie, and then Roman played with Atlas for a little while. All of it seemed a tad odd. With complete honesty, I didn't picture Roman getting along so well with Atlas, all things considered. Admittedly it was cute.

"Julia, come here." A whisper sounded just as I was putting a plate away.

Turning around, no one was waiting for me to answer. A creaking sounded from the basement door opening. The cold air made it's way throughout the living room and kitchen, pricking our skin. Looking over, I saw that Roman and Atlas stared at the door, Roman looking more terrified than Atlas.

"Roman, unfortunately I think that now would be a good time for you to head home."

"What's going to happen?" Concern danced in his tone.

"I imagine nothing good but it's not anything you need to be dragged into. Please Roman, leave." This time, I asked him with more urgency.

"Mom, he's here." Atlas sounded fearful as he stared down the basement stairs.

"Alright love, don't move. Stay there, okay?"

Roman wasn't leaving so I walked over to him and gently started pushing him toward the door which I opened.

"Listen Roman, thank you for coming over tonight, and I'm sorry that my demon problem interrupted the fun. However, I do hope that you had a good time. If I end up surviving yet another night of this demon attack then I'll see you at work tomorrow."

"You'll be okay though, right?" If anything it sounded like he was trying to convince himself that everything would turn out to be well.

"Right, good bye." I was quick and rushed with my response.

Before he could say anything more, I shut the door and turned around to talk to Atlas so we could form a plan. He was nowhere in sight. Worry set in while I couldn't see Atlas.

"Atlas? Come on Atlas, please come here." My voice cracked as Ezekial's words flashed through my mind and the hurt of losing my baby boy once again filled me. The door of the basement slammed shut with such a force it sent a vibration throughout the room. A chill ran down my spine, as my nerves were tightened I released shaky breaths. Every hair on the back of my neck stood up, sending a warning signal to my brain on a mere survival instinct.

"Mom! Mommy help me!" Atlas's blood curdling scream cried out, echoing through the house. His innocent voice was filled with pain and utter terror.

Running over to the basement door praying that my child wouldn't be hurt, my hands gripped the door knob. I jerked violently at it, to no avail. Atlas's screams continued with his pleas for help while I desperately tried at the door. My fists pounded against the wood as I screamed. Tears escaped from my eyes and trailed down to my cheeks.

"Don't hurt him! Do you hear me!? Don't you dare take my child from me or so help me God!"

It was then that the door swung open smacking me to the ground. The light flickered on and off tempting me. Once I got up, I ran down to the basement where Atlas's screams grew louder. Tears poured harder than they ever had in my life as my eyes laid upon the scene that threatened to take all my happiness away from me.

"Atlas!"

My son was surrounded and engulfed in vibrant red flames as he sobbed and cried out to me for help. The demon trailed his long nail down the boy's face as it pierced Atlas's skin, creating a stream of gold liquid to run down his tear stained face. It appeared that he wasn't burning but he sounded like he was in unbearable pain. The demon stood next to him smiling sadistically. I ran as fast as I could to my son, and just as my hand reached out to him and next to the flames, the both of them disappeared. Leaving me, alone, in the cold, barely lit basement with no son. It had ripped my child from me.

"Atlas?" My broken voice filled the lonely air, allowing me no comfort.

"No, no, no, no Atlas. Atlas! Please come back baby, please come back!"

A brokenness filled my soul and crippled me. In just one second, everything was taken from me as a world of pain invaded my heart. My sobs filled the basement as I screamed out for my child, and with it the brokeness bounced off the concrete walls. Part of me died inside while my vision was blurred with tears.

Hope filled me for just a second. Maybe it was a trick. Quickly getting up and yelling out Atlas's name, I searched all the rooms in the house carefully in hopes that he wouldn't be gone, but instead was waiting for me with his dimpled smile. Still tear stricken, I opened up my mother's door. There, she sat her eyes all black along with the same colored veins pulsing from under her skin. No, this was not my mother.

"Give me my son!" My fists balled with anger.

"Julia, I told you that I would take everyone you loved from you until you had no one left and only then would I drag your tortured soul down to hell." His displaced strangled voice erupted from my mother.

"Give me my son!" My voice boomed angrily throughout the room. Her head snapped towards my direction as she got up, and without touching me threw my body to the opposite side of the room, causing me to slam against a dresser.

"In what kind of position do you think you are to request such a thing? Especially to be granted that? Your mother has become very useful these days ever since Salem became useless. I've been slowly weakening her from the inside ever since I took a hold of her to watch you and Atlas. It was far easier that way. She has a very strong will, you know it? No matter, you practically handed the boy to me."

"Please, just give me my son back and leave my mother alone." My broken voice pleaded with him.

"No, that would require a death. Soon, you'll be screaming in hell just like your boy will be." She took large steps to me, grabbing the sides of my head. Her thumbs placed over my open eyes. I could feel her black veins pushing against my naked eye while she applied pressure.

My vision failed me while it began to get blurry. Then, darkness took over.

7 YEARS AGO

"Alright Mrs. Bettington just relax while we put you under anesthesia. The abortion will be over soon. Count to ten for me. Most likely you'll go under at three or five." She sounded so cheerful, so happy as she spoke to me.

"One" Already I felt weird. What dosage did they give me? "Two" After all I did have to pick one of the sketchier places since I'm so far along. "Three" A comfortable blackness lulled me to sleep.

PRESENT TIME

Waking up, my eyes felt heavy. My mother's black veined face immediately fell over me as she held a knife in her hands. Slowly, she raised her hand to stab me. I rolled over right as she plunged the blade down and ran downstairs. Once I reached the bottom floor, I grabbed my keys and ran to my car.

I jumped in, turning the ignition and drove away for what seemed like an hour. I couldn't go back. I needed to figure out how to get my son back and then my mother. No way in hell was I going to let the demon take my child from me and not do anything about it. Where would I go until then? I grabbed my phone and hit the call button, listening to the dialing tone.

"Hello? You didn't die did you? I was worried for you and Atlas." Roman's cheerful voice came through. Bracing myself to be turned down, I spoke.

"Roman, this is incredibly unfair for me to ask this. However, I wouldn't do such a thing unless I was left with no options. Something really terrible happened after you left. Can I please stay at your place for just a night until I formulate my plan?"

"Yeah, sure… are you okay?" I'm assuming he caught my voice crack.

"No." My child is gone.

Roman gave me his address. It was about a 30 minute drive to his house. Pulling in his driveway and walking up to the door, I allowed the rain to fall on my skin as I slowed my pace. The cold bit at my skin while the freezing rain only worked along with it. My body shivered in response to the coldness. I lost my son. My son.

"Jules, if you don't walk any faster you're bound to get sick."

I was so blindly surrounded by my thoughts that I didn't notice the light from his home, nor did I hear his door opening. It illuminated a little of the darkness that wished to consume the night. Hurrying because I was imposing on him already, I went inside. Roman shut the door. How am I going to get my son back? That wasn't a trick. Atlas isn't here anymore. Would he still be here if I hadn't spent so much time saying goodbye to Atlas?

Before I knew it a warm, fuzzy blanket was being wrapped around my shoulders as a tear slipped from my cheek and fell onto my hand. Looking up, Roman was about to hand me a mug of tea to go along with it.

"That'll warm you up. What happened?" Another tear fell.

"He took my child, Atlas's gone. He's suffering and gone. If you would have heard him scream like I did, your heart would be broken as well. My mother's possessed and just tried to murder me. If I don't find a way to get Atlas back, I would sooner die than live without him, again." I turned to look at Roman as I blinked another tear away.

"You'll get him back, and you will figure a way to save your mother as well. Atlas is a very brave and smart kid. I'm sure that he can hold off until you get him. As for your mother, once you get Atlas back that'll seem like a piece of cake."

"Piece of cake?" I asked with disbelief. Flipping through my memories, I only wished to find something of help. Something that would return everything to normal. I can't get Roman into this.

"Thanks for the tea and everything, but I think that it would be better if you stayed away from me. You'll end up dead if you don't."

"Jules, just stay here for a bit, okay? Nothing has happened to me yet, so it's worth it. Just focus on getting your head clear, so you can get your family back. Don't leave until you're a little better." His eyes were filled with sincerity and his voice with urgency.

"Okay." It was all I could respond with my broken voice.

Roman showed me where I would be sleeping and then left me alone after I asked to have a second. Alright, now I have to figure out a plan. I have to get Atlas back. What could I possibly do? Surely, I'll be able to figure it out.

"The paper!" Ezekial said he was trying to help me all along. He didn't attack me! He gave me a clue! Ezekial said go through it.

Looking at the clock on my phone it read that it was two in the morning. Quickly, I wrote a note explaining that I figured it all out to Roman, then left.

Finally after getting to my home, I realized all the lights were turned off. Grabbing my phone, I went up to my door and slowly began to open it. A humming resounded throughout the house. All I have to do is get through, find the paper, draw the symbol, and I'll be okay. I'm doing this for Atlas. Nothing matters more than Atlas.

When I stepped inside, my heart pounded like it would leap out of my chest, leaving no room for any calm. I futilely tried to turn on the lights. No matter how much I flipped them, they refused to cooperate and go on. I used the flashlight from my phone. My steps were slow as I rummaged through the junk drawer, praying I didn't move the paper or throw it away. A creek went on from the opposite side of the room. A loud bang erupted from the darkness behind me. Turning back round, I noticed my saving grace alongside a piece of chalk.

If I'm to go, I need to go now. Someone's hot breath fell on my neck from an inch behind me. I could feel whatever it was looming behind my back. It didn't take me long before I made a run towards the basement door. Halfway there something grabbed my wrist and at a great speed began to drag me up the stairs. When I reached the second step I grabbed onto one of the stairwells and pulled myself in the opposite direction with all my force. This allowed me to escape.

At full speed I ran to the basement, hoping that I would make it. To my surprise, I did exactly that. As my foot touched the first step of the basement stairs, the light to it turned on, but the door slammed shut. The light got brighter and brighter as I took a step down. It got so bright that the mere sight of it pained my eyes. On my second step down, the lights shattered. I tumbled down the stairs and hit my head hard. Another light flickered violently while I tried to focus my blurry vision. Deja Vu caused a bitter chuckle to leave me.

Trying to get up I realized that I lost the piece of chalk on the tumble down. A cry went through the basement. Ignoring it, I searched for the piece of chalk. Looking around I noticed that it was under the stairs. I rose up quickly to retrieve the one thing that I needed to achieve my task. I picked it up and went to one of the walls of the basement and began drawing the symbol from paper.

CHAPTER TWENTY
MOTHER'S LOVE

———◆———

THE HUMMING GOT CLOSER TOWARDS the basement as though someone was in the living room right next to the door. My hands trembled as all of the fear came rushing in like a waterfall. Fear of failing to get Atlas back, fear of whatever was about to unfold, and fear that I would die along with my mother. My mother who tried to murder me, well, the demon in my mother's form. The door to the basement flew off its hinges and shattered, splintering against the concrete wall.

What came next was the exact same form Salem turned into before the cops had come to my house. My mother's limbs were stretched nine feet out and twisted backwards as though the bones snapped. Her jaw was extended by three feet down with her mouth wide open. Black bile dripped from it. The numerous black veins were thick and pulsing all throughout her skin, barely hidden. A loud screech escaped the form as it went down the stairs, coming for me. It ran quickly while I struggled desperately to finish the symbol.

Suddenly, light bursted and everything turned pitch black. The only thing that remained was the sound of the demon on all fours coming towards me at full speed. Before my eyes got a chance to adjust to the gloom, the demon yanked me down and started dragging me away. Just then, a golden outline began to appear on the wall where I drew the symbol. My fingers helplessly clawed against the concrete floor in my attempt to stop myself from being dragged. My fingers pressed so strongly against it that my flesh began to smear off and a few of my nails peeled away like it was nothing.

We neared the stairs just as the symbol turned into a bright gold. Only now, instead of the outline of the symbol it was a hole. The moment it tried to drag me up the first step of the stairs I grabbed onto the side and kicked like my life depended on it, because it did. The demon released me, and I regained my footing. I ran towards the golden hole that was quickly closing on me. The demon trailed close behind.

I jumped into the golden hole which sent me to a fairly unexpected place. The moment I stepped in a sense of loneliness came over me along with sadness. The air was identical to the demon's world. Blackness was all that I could see for miles. The air was so cold that it was suffocating. A baby's cry erupted to my left. There laid a blue baby blanket that had something moving under it. It's cries were pained as I walked towards it.

When I reached the baby, I slowly lifted the blanket away from it's face. Nothing was in it except for a vast amount of blood. My insides twisted in disgust and worry. I have to stay focused. Atlas needs me and I can't let anything distract from that.

"Julia." A faint whisper of a man was slowly let out from behind me. His breath falling on my shoulder.

In response to this familiar voice I turned around to find the demon hunched over. The evil spirit lunged forward at me and knocked me to the ground. The demon seemingly disappeared from my view. Standing up with shaky legs, I wondered how I would reach Atlas. Blood dripped from up above and fell onto my cheek. Looking up, I saw the demon. He dropped onto me and grabbed my face with one of his hands, using the other to plunge his claws into my stomach. The other held my face against the floor.

My cries filled the air as tears gushed from my eyes. He plunged his long nails into my stomach and ripped them out only to do it again. Excruciating pain filled me as I felt his rough nails rake against my insides. Strings of flesh detached themselves as he tore further and further. Although the mass of tears blurred my vision, I could faintly see something black oozing from his nails and when it hit my skin, it burned like acid. The second he plunged his nails into my stomach, again the same burn that I felt from his nails dripping filled my stomach and even though I thought it to be impossible, I felt even greater pain.

As the black liquid ran through and felt like it was burning my insides, I thrashed and twisted with screams of sheer pain. I could feel as the acid like liquid mercilessly burnt through everything in its path. I had cried so much that a small pool of tears laid around my cheeks on the ground. The demon got off of me but his inflicted pain remained. My whole body was soaked in sweat, and my skin burned like I had a fever, but not the same burn that ran through my stomach. Never in my life did I think that such pain existed. The demon leaned down next to my pale face.

"Someone else may have taken your place but that doesn't mean I can't leave you with nothing. I said that I would torture you and so I did. While

I can't drag your tortured soul down to hell, I can cause you to have the incapability to create." The demon's rough, strangled voice filled my ears.

The thought of me dying ran through my mind due to the pain. His words barely reached me since pain consumed all of me, eating away. I won't be able to save Atlas, or my mother either. Pain wasn't the only thing that consumed me, but also regret. Regret from not being able to save the ones I love so dearly. My poor boy. Darkness fell over me, my body giving up on life itself.

CHLOE'S P.O.V.

I woke up on the basement floor feeling terribly sick. Little snippets of what has been going on since Salem came charging at me were barely at my disposal. However, while the demon did take over my body I do remember a lot. My skin crawled thinking of it. It was as though I was in constant pain and felt like I was in the passenger seat while I watched in such disgust as to what the demon was doing. My whole body ached and I felt so weak as the demon ate away at my soul.

Barely being able to stand up, I walked up the stairs thinking. Julia won't be able to defeat the demon. Nor will Atlas. Thankfully I did all the research I could. Oh, I started as soon as they told me everything. It'll be a bitter thing to do but I love my daughter and grand baby with all my heart. I will do everything in my power to save my child along with my grandson.

Unfortunately, I haven't found any other way to do this. However, what must be done, must be done.

A tear escaped my eye as I reached the stairs to get to my room. This has to do it. I walked slowly. All of this will be worth it though. The moment I reached my room I grabbed the rope from my closet and tied it into the correct shape, and then tied it to a hinge in the ceiling. Pulling a chair right below it and climbing up, I put the noose around my neck. All of my research concluded that a sacrifice had to be made. If it is my own life that I must pay for my daughter to live then I will. If this doesn't kill me, the cancer will.

Nerves filled me as I tried to work up the courage to do what must be done in order to save my daughter. All of my memories of her from the day she was born came flooding back in a rush. I'm doing the right thing, I know it.

"Oh my child, Julia, I love you with all my heart. My only regret is all those years I spent away from you. You've done me proud."

I breathed out those words so effortlessly as I took a deep breath in. Making sure to say that I was sacrificing myself in the place of Julia so the demon would hear and leave my daughter alone, I kicked the chair out from under myself. My body instinctively struggled and gasped for air while black dots filled my vision. Slowly, life escaped from out of me as I took my last breath.

CHAPTER TWENTY-ONE

SAFE HAVEN

JULIA'S P.O.V.

"JULIA! YOU DON'T HAVE MUCH time before the portal closes for you to get out. Get up off the ground!"

I opened my eyes to see my father standing before me and trying to help get me up. His efforts failed the moment I moved. The pain from my stomach was unbearable. He looked at my wounds with concern.

"Oh dear, okay Julia, you'll be fine. Just give me a second, okay?"

He laid me back down and looked at me with sorrow as he put his hand over my stomach. A warm, yellow light illuminated from his hand and went through my belly. Screams escaped me as I tried to muffle them by putting my hand over my mouth. That burned like fire. My wounds closing up hurt greatly, not as much as the black liquid. Regardless, it reminded me of what I would see on shows where they would seal a wound with a knife that had been put in the fire for a bit. Such a feeling couldn't compare to Atlas's comfortable healing by golden lights.

"Alright I'm done." My father's words held great love.

He wasted no time whatsoever to help me up from the ground. The only pain that I felt was minor, but I would take it over what I felt a couple minutes ago. We started walking forward for a while before he looked frustrated and teleported us to somewhere else. Where we went was still black and felt the same as before.

"Julia, I'm needed somewhere else right now. I took you as far as I could take you. All you need to do is walk straight just a little bit more and you'll find Atlas. Do you hear me?"

"Yeah, thanks dad."

Before I could tell him that I loved him he was gone. I continued walking forward like he said. It only took a few minutes until I reached Atlas. He was laying on the ground in a fetal position, shaking. Cuts were all over his body, gold liquid leaking from them. I ran over to him immediately.

"Atlas! Are you okay? Talk to me, what's wrong?" I scooped him up into my arms and hugged him tightly. Tears fell from his face as he hugged me back. "What did he do to you?"

"He put me into a fire that took my powers away and kept me caged. He kept cutting me open with his nails. He did that and scared me a lot until he said something about someone taking your place and that he needed to leave you with something." Atlas's voice was shaky and broken.

"I'm so sorry that I left you alone. I'm sorry that I didn't get to you any sooner. I tried really hard to find you. Let's get out of here quickly. My father said the portal is closing."

"It is, I'm sorry I'm not strong enough to hold it for much longer." He sniffled.

"Atlas, don't be sorry. I love you and you did nothing wrong. Come on, we need to hurry."

Atlas and I found our way back and got into the basement. He kept especially close to me, clinging until I picked him up. Once we got upstairs, I told him to go pack some of his things while I searched for something. I hoped to find my mom. The first place I looked was her room. I opened her door hesitantly expecting a demon to jump out at me.

Her body was hanging strung up in the air by her neck. She slowly swung back and forth. Tears brimmed in my eyes as I looked at her lifeless body. I ran to her and tried to get her down but failed. Running to get my phone I called 911. The operator told me they would arrive soon.

"What's wrong?" Atlas asked me when he looked at my face.

"Grandma's gone. I think that is who the demon was talking about. She uhm, she gave herself up to save us."

Atlas started crying with me once I broke the news. We hugged and I tried my best to console him until the sirens were within hearing range. It was odd. I felt as though my whole world was being built back up again since the demon was out of our lives. At the same time it felt like a chunk was missing. The entirety of the situation was bitter sweet. Atlas told me later that mom would be in hell since she sacrificed herself for me. Someone had to go to hell, and it was her on her own account.

Everything after that was a pure blur. It was as though everything escaped me while they asked me questions and declared her dead. No matter how hard I attempted to focus solemnly on what happened concerning her death I was unable to comprehend the events that unfolded in front of me. The only thing I knew was that she was gone, out of my life. A woman who was so involved with me was suddenly gone in the time span of a few moments. That was all it took, a few moments for her to be gone. Such a devastating loss consumed me at every turn.

"What are we going to do now, mom? Mom?" Atlas's soft voice broke into my thoughts despite me wanting the simplicity of solitary. Even though I was mourning, so was Atlas. The boy needed me no matter how unqualified I felt for the task. My reply took a few seconds, given I was in a daze.

"We should move into a different house. I don't like this one anymore." The words fell out with such effort. My hand went up to my cheek as I felt the wetness dripping down, a tear.

"I agree, where will we stay until then?" His head turned to the side at his own question, patiently waiting for my answer.

"My office I guess. Would you be okay with that love?"

"No, that place won't do. I know where you need to be." A smile began to form on his face. However, it wasn't one of great joy like usual or even one of cleverness… reassurance is what his smile revealed.

"Where would that be? A hotel?" My voice seemed much more down than I intended. Come on, I have to be well for Atlas. Atlas is still here and that is enough to be happy about in itself. A smile began to appear on my face as I thought of all the memories with him. I recalled last week when we grabbed the cardboard from the wrapping paper and acted like they were swords.

"Have you really not thought about it, mom? I know you have been busy but still. I could tell you, but then the whole surprise would be ruined. Regardless of what I do or don't do, it's bound to happen. Although, if I do reveal it I can speed the whole process up." He said it with such contemplation.

"What are you talking about?"

"Roman said to you that it's worth it. You don't have a single clue about what he was trying to get through to you?"

"My mind has been a little preoccupied, so no. Whatever it was though, I'm sure it wasn't a big deal. He even said it again before I left his house and came here."

"Mom, come on."

Atlas's small hand encompassed mine while we stood up and he led me to his room. Confusion painted my face, but I chose to remain silent and allow him to show me. When we did get to his room, he pulled something out from under his bed.

"It'll give me energy." The thing he held was golden and slowly disappeared as he held it. Once it was gone he grabbed my hand and smiled the same way he always did when he had a plan.

Without a single warning, we teleported and arrived in a living room. The more I studied it, the more familiarity came rushing back. Atlas stationed us at Roman's. A sense of comfort went through me, but that feeling left just as fast when I really thought about what Atlas just did.

"You just technically broke into Roman's house. That isn't okay. Come on, teleport us back so we can drive to a hotel." Atlas grabbed my hand again and then closed his eyes, only to open them once again.

"Oh no! Look at that! What a shame! You know something, Mom? I don't have the energy. Trust me, I'm just as bothered by this as you are, but I mean we have no other choice of staying here until I get that energy back. Darn, too bad we teleported here instead of driving." Atlas walked over to the bedroom where Roman was letting me stay. "Here's what we should do.

I'll rest up, it's almost six already so I suggest the same to you while I get my energy back. Man, if only we drove here."

Atlas was very obviously lying. He made no attempt to cover up the smile that spread across his face, or his sarcastic tone. Instead of going to sleep I just turned a lamp on and sat down on Roman's couch after grabbing one of his books to read. If I tried to fall asleep my attempts would only fail. What I needed now was a distraction. If a new book could fill my head instead of grief, so be it

ATLAS'S P.O.V.

Teleporting to Roman's room took me a few tries to get the right one. I tried to wake him up but he was like a dead man. This guy could sleep through the apocalypse. Mom needs to realize this so I can tell her my secret. Roman over here needs to realize that if he waits for her to figure it out, she never will. Mom would put such a thing at the bottom of her list. Unfortunately, that's the truth. Roman had a calendar on his wall. Oh!

Hey! It's my birthday soon. I'll be eight! Boy do the years go by. Two weeks before party time!

"Atlas!?" Roman's voice was a quiet yell. He sounded startled but this needed to be said.

"Yes, sorry to wake you like this and coming into your house without permission, but I'm on a mission. My mom is in your living room. Don't be mad at her though, she didn't know I was taking her here so it's just as much a surprise to you as it is to her. Are you going to get up?"

Only then did Roman start to get up. I teleported back to my room, or the room I'm staying in. I'm not sure, but I think Roman went to take a shower because I didn't see him walk out. It's either that or the guy went back to sleep. The suspense almost got to me until I heard his door open.

I teleported to the hallway so I could spy on them without either of them noticing. They were like children I thought. My mission must be completed so I have to stick around here. He did take a shower, his hair was a little wet.

Mom sat there curled up in a chair reading a book. I don't think she heard Roman coming or thought it was me because she made no attempt to turn around as he entered the living room.

Chapter Twenty-Two

Closed Chapter

Julia's P.O.V.

"Atlas, how come you made no attempt to cover up the fact that you could teleport us back? It's one thing to stay here for a couple days, but not as long as you were thinking. I don't think Roman would appreciate us staying here."

"What wouldn't I appreciate?" Roman's voice startled me since I fully expected Atlas to be the one to answer. In fact, I think I overreacted given I jumped up from where I sat and whipped around to face Roman, the book still in my hands.

"I uhm, the, Atlas thinks that we should be staying here while I look for a new place to live." My stammering gave away my unpreparedness.

"Are you okay? Did you take care of the whole demon situation?"

"No, my mother took care of it. She fixed everything at her own cost." My head looked down at the floor as I said the words, wishing that they weren't true.

"Oh, I'm sorry. You are okay though, right?" I looked up back to him. Was I okay? My thoughts trailed back to what the demon said to me. "The incapability to create?" What does that even mean I thought as I said the phrase in my head. Then, it dawned on me. He did it where my stomach is.

"I can't have kids." The words were said quietly under my breath. So quiet, I barely heard myself.

"What?" He looked at me with worry. No, I wasn't okay. My mother was dead, I couldn't have kids of my own, my dog was still back home, and I no longer had a home. I'll spare him the details and having to listen to my problems. Turning the attention around usually works. Typically, the other person forgets the original question at hand.

"Roman, what is it that you meant exactly when you said it's worth it?" He smiled and walked over to me shaking his head. While his face portrayed sureness and amusement, mine was once again filled with confusion. Roman stood close to me and although his face was now completely serious. Seeing Roman serious made me nervous. He always jokes around.

"Jules," He breathed out my name in a way that caused all of my worries to disappear, only Jules wasn't my name.

"Julia." I corrected him with hesitance.

"Julia, I meant that you were worth it. Well, as long as you don't have a demon on your tail." Roman leaned his head down and kissed me. He held me close but with gentleness until we both pulled away. "You avoided my question when I asked you if you were okay." His voice was deep with worry.

"It isn't an easy question to answer. If I were to tell you then I wouldn't be able to distract myself."

"I'll make you a pot of tea then."

Roman and I watched a comedy movie on his couch and drank tea while he did his best to make me laugh. Most of the time, he succeeded. After what I assume was an hour, I fell asleep. Later, I had woken up in the room that I was staying in and went outside to find Atlas. He winked at me after he saw me and then giggled. Atlas knew something.

"What do you know?"

"I know that you and Roman talked."

"How much did you see?"

"I teleported away after he went to kiss you. I don't wanna see that." Atlas acted like he was going to throw up after he said it in disgust. "After that I went to see if he had any food, and you guys were watching a movie, but then he had to carry you to bed because you fell asleep. Can I tell you the secret now? I'll just tell you. You once asked me why is it that some people can see me while others cannot. Only my family can see me. Salem was an exception since she had some demon power in her."

"Roman isn't your father though."

"I know, but you guys have a future so it counts." Atlas didn't seem bothered by the least bit, so I smiled.

"Good to know." I gave him a wink as I ruffled his hair.

FIVE YEARS LATER

"Mommy look! I got all these flowers for you, see!" Rose's face was filled with joy. Her long auburn hair and green eyes shined in the sun. Since she was only five Rose's voice was small but filled with life and joy.

"Rose! Those are so beautiful, thank you love." She gave me a hug and skipped away in the grass. Rose was always so bubbly.

"Matthew and Atlas! Don't be so harsh with one another!" I yelled out to my sons who were wrestling too violently for my liking. Matthew had black hair and blue eyes. It always amazed me how little Rose and Matthew looked nothing alike considering they were twins. Obviously, I didn't think they would look the same since they aren't identical ones, but still.

Roman's car pulled into the driveway, the gravel crunched from under the tires as I got up from the chair outside and set aside my book. The kids rushed and all jumped on him. For a second, Roman lost his balance and looked like he was going to fall.

"Alright guys, get off your dad and wash up, it's time for dinner." Dinner was simple leftover spaghetti. They all ran inside like it was a race, coming close to knocking Rose down. Roman caught up with me and put his arm around my waist as we walked into the kitchen.

"How was your day?" He always asked that question right when he got home from work, not that I minded.

"It was good, but Matthew and Atlas are getting too rough when they wrestle. Matthew almost got hurt."

"They're boys, Jules, It'll be okay. I promise. I'll fix you your plate while you get everyone else's."

"Thank you."

"Before I do that though…" Roman turned me around and gave me a kiss. Only then did he proceed to make me my plate. We stood in silence while we both worked. Glancing over at the kids, I felt something missing. I wished to adopt more children. We adopted Rose and Matthew when they were two and although they were my bunches of joy including Atlas, I still would like to expand my family.

"You know I was thinking. I want some more kids." Roman's voice broke the silence as though he was reading my mind. At this, my face lit up.

"Me too! I want to have another daughter and son! However, I think we should adopt a girl first and then adopt another boy a couple years after that. Three boys, and two girls sounds absolutely perfect along with a husband." Roman smiled brightly at me.

"I couldn't agree more with you, love."

A demon who will stop at nothing to make Julia Bettington's life a living hell begins to inflict a series of twisted events on her. The entity strips everything Julia takes joy in, aiming to make her each waking second an excruciating misery. As it wishes to torture her and take her every last breath, a little boy enters her life swearing to fight off the demon and save her. While Julia struggles to keep her soul, she starts to uncover the secrets of the little boy who nudged his way into her life.

Printed in the United States
by Baker & Taylor Publisher Services